Misbooked for Love

MARIA RIGOU

AUTHOR'S NOTE

Misbooked for Love is an open door romance. This means that it has on-page sexual content between two consenting adults. There is use of profanity and explicit language throughout the story. Mature readers only. **Please read with care.**

———

If you enjoy reading *Misbooked for Love*, I urge you to leave a review on Goodreads, Amazon or The Storygraph. Reviews allow indie authors like me to be seen by more readers, so the more, the merrier.

Happy reading!

ABOUT THE COVER

The spectacular cover for *Misbooked for Love* was created by Nysha Lilly.

Nysha was an extremely talented artist and really nailed the vibes I was going for for Clara and Tom's story. Unfortunately, Nysha passed away very unexpectedly in November 2024, leaving behind a son who she adored.

For more information about Nysha Lilly's work, her Instagram profile remains open @nyshalilly.

*For those who believe that love, in all its imperfect beauty,
is always worth the leap.*

And for my sister, Clara.

1

CLARA

THE COLD IS the first thing that hits me. Icy and sharp and right in my eyes.

I wrap my scarf tightly around my neck and draw in a sharp breath. My lungs immediately fill with crisp, freezing air. It's nothing like I've experienced before—the winters I know back in Argentina are humid and warmer, not like this dry, seeping cold that cuts through to my bones and bounces around inside my skull.

There's a golden glow illuminating the buildings in the distance; twinkling lights are starting to shine in the early light of dusk, draped from bare tree trunk to bare tree trunk in the plaza I can see from where I'm standing.

It's already stunning, breathtaking, and I didn't even get to see the mountain yet. My heart responds in kind—a level of excitement I haven't felt in years, probably since my first flight as a flight attendant—fluttery nerves that make me giddy with anticipation.

Everything is white, covered in snow and looking so much like a picture that...it's magical, and the sigh that leaves my lips is nothing short of dramatic. *But in a good way.* A great way, even.

The best way.

This place feels like something out of those corny Christmas movies, the kind I used to watch late at night growing up, while wrapped in a blanket with the air conditioning at full blast, pretending it was winter and snowing outside. Even though, for us, Christmas was in the dead of summer, and unless something apocalyptic happened, snow wasn't ever in the forecast.

The closest I've ever been to touching snow is the frozen morning dew on a bitter winter morning in the city, but that doesn't even last enough to count.

I take a hesitant step forward from the shuttle towards the hotel entrance, and my boot sinks into the fresh snow with a soft crunch. A shiver runs up my spine—not only from the cold, but from the thrill of being somewhere so unfamiliar, so utterly different from what I've known until now.

Snow. Actual snow. I want to laugh at how ridiculous I must look, a woman in her mid-thirties, standing here, gaping at frozen water like I've never seen a winter in my life. I haven't. Not like this, at least.

I look around, trying to take it all in. The Canadian mountains loom big in the distance, not too far from where the small plaza ends, their peaks dusted with white and fading into a dusky sky. Somewhere nearby, the sound of laughter mingles with a constant thud, a noise I've never heard before and can't place. A couple walks past me and into the hotel's revolving door, their cheeks flushed red from the cold, holding hands and giggling like they've just shared a naughty secret.

I steady myself, taking another deep, cold breath, and forge ahead toward the main lodge where I can see the warm, welcoming glow of the entrance.

Inside, the air is thick with the scent of vanilla and flowers. A large fireplace, probably five stories high, dominates one side of the lobby, and clusters of guests sit in oversized chairs in the main sitting area, sipping warm drinks and chatting. Quite literally like a movie. It's lovely.

"Hi there!" There's a chirp behind me that interrupts my ogling, and I turn to see a uniformed attendant waving at me on the other side of a large wooden desk. "Welcome to Sugar Peak Resort," she greets, her voice a warm polarity to the chill outside. "Checking in?"

"Yes," I say, trying to sound casual, though my breath still comes out in little puffs, clearly the contrast between the hellish summer I left behind in Argentina and the cold winter wreaking havoc on my body. "Clara Ledesma."

"Let me just find your reservation." She hums and taps a few keys on her computer, her polite smile never leaving her face. "Ah, here we are," she says, dropping her sunny voice with the last syllable and blinking a few times. I stare at her, not completely understanding her expression. "Looks like you're staying in villa fourteen, one of our coziest spots!" she continues with that big customer service smile again, making me a little dizzy with all the flip-flopping expressions. "You're in for a treat. The view of the mountain from there is to die for!"

I can't help the grin that spreads across my face, regardless of that small moment of doubt she made me have. "I'm excited."

The receptionist—Laura, as her name tag reads—hands me a key card. "We have a Winter Wonderland bonfire tonight on the main terrace, right through those doors." She gestures with her hand, her eyes set on a pair of sliding glass doors towards the end of the building. "Hot chocolate, marshmallows, live music... It's a lot of fun if you're interested. And don't worry, there's plenty of outdoor heating, so you'll be comfortable all night." She chuckles, turning her head back to me. "First time in the snow?"

"What gave it away?" I ask with a smile, dragging my hand through the long hair that is poking out of my hat. But I stop for a moment—maybe my face is more telling than I thought. It was a horrible year for me, and this is my chance to get away, disconnect from my actual life and find...what's missing.

Laura nods with a grin. "Don't worry, you're not the only one. We get a lot of first-timers here, especially this time of the year. You'll blend right in."

I laugh and grab my suitcase, feeling that little flutter in my chest again. Maybe I did make the right call, coming here to start fresh after that string of... Whatever that was.

The past few years weren't any better either. And it all started when my boyfriend of many years, who I'd been living with, broke up with me out of the blue. One day we were together, in his hometown, about to celebrate his grandmother's milestone birthday. The next, I was on a bus returning to Buenos Aires and moving out of the apartment we shared, running back to my parents' house until I could figure it out.

"Just wait until you see it at night, completely lit up." She sighs, a soft smile on her lips. "Now, if you need anything, just give us a call. And enjoy your stay."

"Thank you," I say, and head towards the hallway, following the sign for the villas, my large suitcase clunking along the polished wooden floor beneath me. I can't stop smiling as I pass by the floor-to-ceiling windows, catching glimpses of the slopes outside, bathed in the golden glow of the setting sun. There are no skiers on the mountains, and instead large machinery is grooming the hills, moving up and down, flattening the snow and making it look pristine.

Villa fourteen is towards the end of the hallway, tucked right where the building turns a corner to the right and it continues, doors on either side of the walls, numbered up to twenty. The door clicks open, and I step inside, greeted by a rush of warm air. The room is even cozier than I'd imagined—soft, earthy tones, a stone fireplace that crackles gently in the middle of the living room and big, fluffy throws draped over a large leather sofa that looks the right amount of worn-in and comfy as can be. And the view... I walk over to the window, my breath catching as I look out at the snow-covered hills, the trees dusted with white, and the town's lights twinkling below.

"This is good," I whisper to myself, feeling the tension from the past few months starting to melt away. This is exactly what I need. A fresh start. A break from everything. A turn in my luck. Maybe coming here on a whim isn't such a terrible idea after all. So far, things are looking up. Much better than they've been for the past few years.

My phone buzzes in my purse, jolting me from my thoughts. I pull it out and see *Mamá* on the screen, but I hesitate for a moment before answering, because I know exactly what's coming.

"*Hola, Ma,*" I say, smiling as I greet her. The woman has an uncanny ability to detect bullshit. It made for very difficult teenage years, because when all my friends were going out clubbing at seventeen and lying to their parents, I was stuck at home. It wasn't bad, not at all, but sometimes I wish I'd been a little more rebellious.

"Clarita," she says, a sigh catching on her lips. As if she has been waiting with bated breath for me to let her know I arrived. "Did you arrive safely? Is everything okay? Are you warm enough?" Her voice is filled with concern, which only makes me smile more. Ever since I moved back in with them, she's been just far enough not to hover but close enough to be there, immediately, if I need her.

"Just walked into my room," I say, turning on my heels and looking around. There's a staircase to the left of the kitchen, and by the looks of it from down here, there's at least one bedroom on the second level and a few other doors that look like they could be closets or bathrooms. The island is big enough to sit six, the dark stone countertops reflecting the overhead light. It's masculine and modern, slightly industrial, but at the same time cozy and warm, like a hot cup of coffee on a cool, crisp morning. "I think I could ski out of this room. It has a little patio outside and it's literally a step away from the snow."

"I still can't believe you went all the way to that ski resort in Canada by yourself," she says, like every single day for the past week since I decided to take this trip. "Are you sure this is what you need?"

"*Ma,*" I whisper into the phone, dragging my suitcase with me towards the stairs. "*Ya lo hablamos.*" Yes, it's exactly what I need. A little adventure, something new, to get me out of that funk and out of your house. And to be as far away as possible from Argentina. But I don't say that, because she'll worry. Instead, I roll my eyes affectionately and chuckle. "But honestly, it's so nice here."

She sighs, not convinced. "I just don't want you to be alone, especially after... you know. Everything."

That *everything* she's talking about is the string of breakups I've had since my relationship with Santiago Williams—the longest I've ever had—ended three years ago. And one day, I woke up with the sudden urge to explore and see things I'd never seen before and booked a trip to the middle of the mountains to a ski resort because, honestly, it was a great use of the thousands of points I had accumulated, but also because I wanted to be very far away, hoping the distance would help sort my feelings out.

"*Mami,* that's the whole point."

"Bueno está bien," she relents, though I can hear the worry still lacing her voice. "Just be careful and keep warm and call me tomorrow, okay? It's late here."

"We can FaceTime and I can show you the mountain."

"Chau, hija."

I hang up and stare at the phone for a moment before tucking it away and heading up the stairs, dragging, yet again, the giant suitcase that's been following me for the past twenty-four hours. "Alright, we got this. A little adventure. This will be perfect."

Once in the room, I pull out all my clothes and put them away neatly, using half of the dresser drawers and one side of the walk-in closet. I'm not sure who vacations here, but the bedroom is huge—a large bed in the middle and a walk-in closet the size of my bedroom back home. I'm staying for twelve days, an *excessive amount,* according to my mother, and I want to be comfortable. And if I've learned anything from all my years as a flight attendant, it's that unpacking makes even the shortest of stays feel like a luxury vacation instead of a thirteen-hour layover in an airport hotel.

My winter clothes—or rather, the borrowed stuff I was able to collect from my group of friends—sits at the bottom of the suitcase. Thermal leggings, three thick sweaters, an extra pair of gloves, a few options for hats and a long jacket that looks more like a sleeping bag than a coat that I still don't know how to properly zip, but which promises I'll be warm enough in this crazy climate.

After a few minutes of wrestling with the layers, I finally manage to get everything on, looking like a puffed-up red balloon in the process. My cheeks are pink and my hair is both matted and staticky at the same time, and I make a mental note to take a long bath after I find something to eat.

The hotel is big, and the hallway the villas are in seems endless. I decide to walk in the opposite direction I came in, hoping that at some point I can find an exit and I don't have to walk all the way back to the hotel's lobby. There's a family with young kids entering their room up ahead, the luggage cart overflowing with suitcases and skis and grocery bags filled with food. The two small children are jumping up and down, impatiently waiting for their father to open the room door.

I'm distracted by the little girl in two tiny braids, hugging a small stuffed pig, and I bump into a tall, broad-shouldered man who is heading in my direction. He is mid-conversation on his phone, his voice low and soft. "I know…"

"Sorry," I stammer, taking a step back, feeling my cheeks flush from more than just the heat in the hallway.

He glances at me briefly, his expression annoyed.

"More careful," he mutters, his focus back on his call, brushing past me without another word.

I watch him disappear around the corner, my annoyance flaring, but quickly dissolving because I'm suddenly so hungry that my stomach starts making loud noises.

I'll make friends tomorrow.

2

TOM

THE RESORT LOBBY IS WARM, decorated with heart-shaped garlands and red and pink ribbons every-where, the kind of festive cheer that usually makes people smile. But I'm not smiling. I stand at the check-in desk, tapping my fingers impatiently on the counter as the receptionist, a cheerful woman with a light-up heart necklace, fumbles with my reservation.

"Thomas Hall, right?" she says, her tone bright, like she's determined to spread her Valentine's Day cheer no matter what. "Thomas Edward Hall, III?"

"That's me," I reply, trying to force what I think could pass as a smile. Inside, though, I'm fuming. This skiing trip was supposed to be a chance to reconnect with Ellie, to make up for all the missed weeks that

I've been traveling for work. But she's stuck on the other side of the continent, snowed in at her mother's house in New York, and I'm here alone, surrounded by happy families and couples holding hands.

The receptionist slides my key card across the desk. "You're in villa fourteen, just down this hall." She makes a gesture with her hand, indicating the right way to go. "You'll have a great view of the slopes, and the ski lift is just a short walk away. But your villa has ski-in, ski-out privileges, so you can opt for that if it's your preference." She smiles. "We have a bonfire tonight on the terrace—hot cocoa, marshmallows, the works. Valet will take your remaining luggage to your room, and your ski gear will be stored downstairs in our rental shop. If you'd like for it to be brought up in the morning, just give us a call."

"Okay, thanks," I mutter, picking up the key. I grab my carry-on bag and make my way down the hallway, trying not to let the love songs playing softly through the speakers get under my skin. One side of the hall is lined with black-and-white photos of skiers and snowboarders, a vintage feel to the space. There are a few young children photographed, probably in the sixties or seventies, sliding down one of the tall runs, the ski lift running parallel to them. All I can think about is how Ellie was supposed to be here, right beside me, her first real ski trip.

I feel the vibration of my cellphone in my pocket,

so I stop for a moment to grab it. I don't have to look at the screen to know it's Erin, my ex, calling so I can talk to my daughter.

"Hey, honey," I say, trying to keep the disappointment from my voice. She's going to be bummed, but the least I can do is show her that there's nothing we can do about things out of our control, so we have to take them in stride. I'll definitely make it up to her once we're on the same coast. Maybe I'll get her a puppy, since she's been asking for months.

"Hey, Dad." Ellie's voice is bright, despite the circumstances, and it tugs at something right in my chest. "We're snowed in."

"I know," I say, and not a second later something bumps against me, making me stop in the middle of the hallway. Ellie is babbling about something or other, but I can only look at the stunning woman in front of me, blushing furiously, the color of her cheeks matching her bright red coat.

"Sorry," she says, and I'm startled, blinking repeatedly because I can't really understand what is happening. Her long, blond hair pokes out of her pink Fair Isle hat, and her blue eyes are huge, wide open and observing me.

"I need to be more careful," I say to get away, and give her a small nod, quickly walking past her in the direction of my room, just a few doors ahead, right where the building turns a corner.

The villa is big, a little bigger than we needed, but as soon as I saw the pictures I knew Ellie would have loved it. The kind of place that makes you want to curl up and watch a movie and forget about the world outside. There is a stone fireplace in the middle of the living room, and the view from the large window is exactly as promised: sweeping, snow-covered slopes, the sun just beginning to set behind the mountains. I leave my bag by the entry bench and glance around; there is a door to a half bath under the stairs and nothing else here except the giant open-concept space. The full kitchen is to my right, with an oversized island that I've only seen in magazines and a live-edge dining table that accommodates at least twelve people.

"Did you make it to the grocery store before everything shut down?" I ask, hoping to keep her on the phone just a little longer, partially selfish of me because I don't want to be alone with my thoughts. The fridge is stocked with everything I requested: eggs, milk, cold cuts and Ellie's favorite fruits and veggies.

"We did," she says enthusiastically. "Mom bought us so much hot chocolate, it's ridiculous. We've been drinking it all day." She pauses, and I can hear the faint sound of her mom calling in the background, asking if she wants more marshmallows.

I make my way up the stairs, phone in one hand and bag in the other, looking for the bedroom and bathroom so I can wash the travel away. "It's really snowy, Dad. The plows can't even get down our street yet."

Once in the bedroom, I run a hand through my hair and take a deep breath, forcing myself to focus. This wasn't how I pictured things, but I'll make the best of it. I stare out at the mountain, my jaw tightening. "Yeah, I heard. I'm sorry, honey. I really wanted us to have this time together."

"I know," she replies. Her voice is small, and I can tell she's trying to sound grown-up, trying not to let on how disappointed she is. "It's okay, though. We'll do it another time, right?"

"Absolutely."

These are the moments when I hate my profession. After retiring from playing polo, I partnered with a former player to start breeding horses. The season ended a few months ago and this is when my work picks up, right after the holidays. It's not rare for me to travel for weeks at a time, but the older Ellie gets, the more she notices my absence and the more it weighs on me. Erin has been wonderful about it, but it's getting difficult for all of us. Because the more I get into this, the more competitive I realize this business is. There are high standards in polo ponies, and I don't think this is for me—both the time it needs, and the work and effort we need to put into it.

"As soon as I'm back from this trip, we'll find

another weekend. Just you and me, I promise." I rub the back of my neck, guilt weighing heavy. I've promised her so many things this year, and most of them have fallen through, and maybe this is the straw that breaks the horse's back, pun intended. "I miss you, honey," I say, the words coming out quieter than I want them to.

"I miss you too, Dad," she replies softly. "You better not get too good at skiing without me."

I laugh, but it's forced, empty. "Don't worry, I'll be terrible. No fun without you here to keep me on my toes."

My nine-year-old giggles, and it's the kind of sound that makes everything feel lighter, even if just for a moment. But when she says goodbye and hangs up, the room feels emptier than before. I sit on the edge of the bed, staring at the phone in my hand, the screen already dark.

This trip was supposed to be my shot at making up for lost time and figuring out what I want to do with my time moving forward. Now it's just another reminder of how much I've missed and will continue to miss if things stay like this, if I don't make the necessary changes to untangle my messy life. All the traveling is taking a toll on my relationships, and I can't seem to find joy in the work that I do. I loved the sport, the rush of adrenaline it gave me, being outside the larger part of the year, spending time with those wonderful beasts. But the transition to being behind the scenes has been rough, and I'm looking for a change.

I stand up and open my bag, rummaging through its contents until I find what I want. The set of Valentine's Day pajamas I bought for Ellie are still on top, no longer folded neatly waiting for her. My own clothes get tossed onto the corner chair, landing somewhere I can't see in the dark. The sun has dipped behind the mountain and the sky is quickly darkening, the town coming alive under twinkling lights.

In the bathroom, I strip off my clothes, leaving them in a pile on the floor, and turn on the shower. The steam fills the oversized space quickly, fogging up the mirror, and I step under the spray, letting the hot water hit my back. I stand there for a long time, trying to let the heat wash away my frustration, but it clings to me, stubborn and unyielding.

I scrub a hand over my face and sigh. After a while, I shut off the water, grab a towel, and dry off. My thoughts are still tangled and frayed and wrapped in a guilt that doesn't seem to want to leave, instead clinging tightly like a toddler would to a parent on the first day of school.

I wrap the towel around my waist, water dripping from my hair, and step out of the bathroom, ready to flop down on the bed and figure out what the hell I'm going to do with myself for the rest of this trip. I could always fly back once the storm on the East Coast passes, but—

But I freeze.

There's a woman standing in the middle of my room. Tall, blonde hair pulled into a messy bun, and she's halfway through shrugging off a thick white sweater that makes her look like a bundled-up marshmallow. For a split second, I think I'm hallucinating. Then she turns, and her blue eyes go wide, her face flushing a deep crimson.

"Oh my god!" She gasps, clutching the sweater against her chest, like it'll somehow shield her from this absurd situation. "I'm so sorry—I thought this was my villa! Why would the door open if this wasn't my villa? Oh, god." Her accent is thick, and her voice rises in a panicked jumble of English and what I'm almost certain is Spanish as she fumbles backward, nearly tripping over my shoes by the door.

"What the hell?" I manage to say, my brain finally catching up to the scene unfolding in front of me. I yank the towel tighter around my waist, still dripping wet, and glance around, trying to piece together how exactly this random woman ended up in my room.

"I—I just... I thought it was my room," she repeats, her eyes darting everywhere but at me. "I was in fourteen but... oh, god, is this fourteen? I can't believe—*¡Qué vergüenza!*" She claps a hand over her mouth, clearly mortified.

But I can't speak. Instead, I'm staring at her, opening and closing my mouth like a fish out of water, trying to catch its breath and figure out how to live. This whole situation is surreal, like something out of a bad sitcom.

The woman starts moving but then stops abruptly.

"Wait a second," she says, looking around. She reaches the dresser and yanks it open, the forceful movement making the television on top move precariously. I run a hand through my hair, water droplets scattering onto the floor. And she starts to laugh, a high, nervous sound that only makes the moment more awkward. "It seems you are the intruder."

She gestures with her hand to the drawer, filled with colorful clothing that definitely does not belong to me.

"Huh?" I finally say, like the idiot I'm sure I am. I try to understand what she's inferring, but I can't. Maybe it's the long travel day catching up to me. Maybe it's her—her energy and her spunk and her laughter in this moment, so disarming that I can't focus.

She raises an eyebrow, and the corner of my mouth twitches, despite the confusion and my half naked state. I should be appalled, really. But now I'm intrigued.

"Is this how you introduce yourself to all your neighbors?" she asks, one hand on her hip in the most cocky way. "Most people start with a friendly wave, maybe a plate of cookies. Not a strip show."

I groan and bury my face in one of my hands. "Why is this happening to me?" I mumble behind the palm of my hand. Clearly things have to start getting better. Can't be worse than this.

"You know what?" she says, and her eyes finally find mine. There's a slight blush on her cheeks still, but her expression shifts and her gaze turns deadly. "Oh no, oh no. No, no. It's you."

"Me?"

"Oh, the rude jerk that bumped against me in the hallway and didn't even apologize. Nope. You know what?"

I blink, unable to come up with a response. Is this a rhetorical question? Am I supposed to answer her now?

She turns on her heel and runs down the stairs. I hear the slam of the door below, and I stand there for a moment, still dripping, the towel slipping slightly at my waist. My heart's pounding—not just from the surprise, but from the absurdity of it all.

"What the fuck," I mutter, walking into the closet and seeing at least five outfits hanging from the rod, stacks of neatly folder shirts and sweaters on the shelves on one side of the closet. "Fuck."

3

CLARA

I PRACTICALLY FLY DOWN the hallway, my cheeks burning from the embarrassment of what just happened. My heart is pounding, and my mind is still reeling from the sight of that gorgeous man, half naked, dripping wet, and glaring at me like I was in the wrong. I barrel past a group of teenagers taking selfies in front of a giant heart-shaped wreath by the door, my boots squeaking against the polished wooden floors as I make my way back to the front desk.

The receptionist from this afternoon is still there, except now she's wearing a light-up heart necklace that, frankly, looks ridiculous. She looks up, startled as I skid to a stop in front of her. Her smile is polite but a little deprecating, as if I were a lost puppy trying to find its way home. And it only makes my irritation spike.

"Hi, um, Laura," I say, squinting at her name tag while I'm violently blinded by her glowing necklace. "Excuse me." I'm breathless and fumbling over my words. "There is a man in my villa. A man who is not supposed to be there."

She blinks, her smile faltering. "Oh... I'm sorry, could you clarify—"

"I just walked into my villa—villa fourteen, the one you checked me into—and... and found a man. Naked. Well, almost naked. In my room. In my bathroom. Using the towel I was planning to use tonight after a long bath. I need a bath." I wave my hands, trying to get my point across without bursting into hysterical laughter at the absurdity of it all. "I mean, why would he be there if it's my villa?"

Her eyes widen, and she clicks around on her computer, the screen reflecting off her heart necklace in frantic little flashes. "Oh my goodness," she says, cocking her head to the side, analyzing whatever is on the screen in front of her. "I'm so sorry about that. Let me just pull up your reservation details again."

I stand there, bouncing on the balls of my feet, my mind replaying the mortifying scene of the man wrapped in that towel, his broad shoulders dripping water all over the floor. He looked furious, and honestly, I don't blame him. But it's not my fault. I booked this room fair and square. With the hundreds of thousands of points I've accumulated throughout my years traveling. Yes, it's mine. And I deserve it because it's been hell for the past three years, and I just need space and time and to be freaking alone.

"There's clearly been some sort of mistake," I add, trying to sound calm but failing miserably. "I was told it was my villa. You checked me in! I came here to relax, not share my space with some asshole—" I cut myself off, realizing I'm venting to the wrong person and this is not what she needs right now.

Laura the receptionist looks up, her face apologetic and white as a ghost. "I'm so sorry, Ms. Ledesma. It seems there was an error in our system." She looks back down at her screen and tap, tap, taps her keyboard a few times, hemming and hawing. "It seems," she repeats, "we double-booked villa fourteen."

She finally looks up at me and blinks a few times, expectant.

"Okay," I drawl, trying to get the conversation moving. I have no answer for her. I'm expecting a solution to come from her lips any second now.

The man, that disgustingly good-looking asshole that I had the dishonor of looking at half naked just now, chooses that very moment to walk up, his thick thighs encased in gray sweatpants and his lean torso covered in a long sleeve white shirt. He's walking in the direction of the front desk, a stoic look on his face and his stride casual and slow, like this is not a problem at all.

"And, it seems, unfortunately, because of the Valentine's Day weekend and the snowstorm, all of our other accommodations are currently full."

I stare at her, uncomprehending. "What do you mean, full? Like, completely full?"

"Yes," she says with an apologetic wince. "Every villa, every room. We've had so many unexpected guests due to the storm back east, and with the holiday weekend... I'm really, truly sorry."

"Wait, what storm? You know what? Not important right now." I shake my head and close my eyes, taking a deep, calming, centering breath. "So you're telling me that I'm stuck sharing with—" I gesture vaguely in the direction of this guy, who is now standing next to me and looking at the heart-shaped necklace like it offends him. My frustration bubbles over. "I mean, I don't even know him! He could be anyone!"

"I'm right here," he replies, crossing his arms, his muscles bunching up with the movement. "And I can say the same thing about you, too."

"Oh! Mr. Hall, Tom!" She nods enthusiastically at him, her heart necklace moving along with her. "I'm so sorry for the confusion, sir," she adds, looking straight at him with the biggest smile ever displayed by a human being. And I would know, I work with people all day long.

"We've already comped your resort fee, and we're happy to offer complimentary services—spa access, meal vouchers, anything we can do to make this right," she continues, her voice earnest. "But unfortunately, as far as lodging goes, there's no other option at the moment."

"Can you call any of the other properties in town? I mean, *someone* has to have at least one room."

"Let me see what I can do." My shoulders slump, and Laura retreats to a back office, her steps hurried and urgent. This was supposed to be my solo getaway, my chance to clear my head and figure out what the hell I'm doing with my life. Instead, I'm sharing my space with a stranger who already seems to hate me. This is what I get for even thinking things were looking up. I can hear the man's breathing next to me, his fingers tapping on the reception desk with a completely random tempo.

"I'm Clara," I mumble, avoiding his gaze because I really don't want to be here. It's obvious he doesn't either, but we have to start somewhere, especially the way it's looking right now.

"Thomas," he says, lifting his hand in a lazy wave. "Tom. I'm Tom." And as soon as the last letter of his name is out of his mouth, his hand goes back to tapping on the flat surface in front of him. The moment is tense, and at least for me, I'm wishing and hoping there's a solution. I imagine it's the same for him, if only because sharing a room with a complete stranger is not ideal.

But as soon as the receptionist comes back, only a few minutes later, her face tells me everything I need to know. "Fine," I mutter, rubbing my temples and not letting her give me the bad news. "This is not how I pictured spending my vacation." Just my luck.

Laura nods, her expression genuinely sympathetic. "I completely understand. If anything changes, you'll be the first to know. But for now..." She trails off, helpless.

I give her a tight smile and turn away, heading back down the hall with a knot in my stomach. Sharing my space with a man—with anyone!—wasn't on my agenda, and every step I take back towards my room feels like I'm marching down to my own personal hell. Especially because the goal of this trip is to spend time with myself to try to figure out what is next.

———

The door creaks when I open it, and I peek inside with caution, half expecting to find the man still half naked and fuming in the living room, even though I just saw him fully clothed in the lobby thirty minutes ago. But he's not. I take a hesitant step inside, glancing around. The space looks the same as it did when I first arrived —cozy, with a giant fireplace and an oversized sofa that is practically begging for someone to curl up on it and forget the world exists outside of this mountain bubble. Except now, my problems are very much here, cohabitating with me.

I spot him sitting at the kitchen island, his hair now completely dry and mussed as if he'd run his fingers through it relentlessly. After the conversation with the receptionist and my abrupt walking away, I sat by the giant fireplace in the lobby and looked into the fire. I guess he made it back to the room before I did, and now he's scrolling through his phone, clearly tense. The moment he hears me, he looks up, his expression something I can absolutely decipher after years in customer-facing roles. He's annoyed as fuck. And he should be, of course. But it's not my fault.

"They messed up," I say, my voice sharper than how I planned it in my head. "They double-booked, and apparently there's not a single open room in this whole town for me to move to." I toss my sweater on the counter, my irritation flaring up again just looking at him. "So, unless you've got a magic solution, it looks like we're stuck."

"I know. I was there." He sighs, setting his phone down and closing his eyes slowly. One of his hands twitches on the island, as if he wants to grab something and throw it to the floor in a classic temper tantrum. "Great. Just great." He runs a hand through his hair, tousling the brown locks. "I was supposed to have this place to myself."

"Yeah, well, I was supposed to have this place to myself, too. So, now what?"

The man exhales slowly, his frustration palpable. "Look, I don't like this any more than you do. But I don't have anywhere else to go, and clearly, neither do you. So let's figure this out."

We stare at each other, two strangers forced into a ridiculous situation. The tension between us feels like it could snap at any moment. Finally, Tom leans back, crossing his arms, and oh boy, the muscles again. I was not prepared for such a sight, and I've seen this man half naked, for crying out loud!

"Listen, Clara," he says. "It's a big villa. I'll just take the room and I'll make sure to stay out of your hair. You do your thing, I'll do mine. Easy."

"Easy," I repeat, lifting one shoulder casually, in the most nonchalant way I know how. Even though I'm feeling very chalant right now. I stand a little straighter, folding my arms to match his stance. "Except that I was here first, so you know, the room is mine."

He raises an eyebrow but nods. "Okay."

All right, easy it is, it seems.

"And I like to have breakfast alone," I blurt out

quickly. "It's my thing." I inwardly cringe, because that's not even remotely true, but just his mere energy makes me want to have the last word.

He snorts, though there's no real humor behind it. "Fine."

I stare at him. More like glare. And he responds in kind, his light brown eyes studying my face intently. His gaze moves from my eyes to my lips, then back, blinking for a moment before looking away.

He's handsome. In that *rugged*, I work behind a desk and get paid good money to say things like *circle back*, and *we need alignment*, and *make sure you secure the funds* way. I want to snort at my own joke, because there's nothing rugged about him, but there's totally a corporate, *finance bro* vibe emanating from those muscles.

And then I catch myself looking at him with my stupid, dangerous heart eyes, and I stop. Because this is what happens to me, and then disaster comes knocking. So instead, I huff and turn around, frustrated at myself, and make really sure I get the last word in. "Yep, take it or leave it, my dude."

4

CLARA

MY BODY IS FREEZING COLD. The kind that creeps into your bones, that pulls you out of a deep sleep and forces you to pay attention to the way your toes are curling up for warmth. I tug the blanket tighter around myself, but that does nothing to help. Every breath I take is visible in the dim moonlight filtering through the curtains, as if I'd forgotten the actual window open instead of the blackout drapes. I blink into the darkness, and it takes a minute before I realize what is wrong.

My room feels like a freezer.

I lie there for a second, groggy and disoriented, trying to figure out if I'm still dreaming. But when I exhale again and see another puff of my breath in the air, I know I'm not. I shiver as I sit up, the cold air biting at my skin like I'm outside in the snow rather than wrapped up in the most comfortable bed I've slept in in years. My fingers fumble for my phone on the nightstand, and the clock reads 2:14 AM.

Wonderful.

The blanket offers no relief from the biting chill, so I throw on my cardigan and grab my wool socks from the floor, yanking them on with cold, clumsy hands. The villa is silent except for the distant hum of a fan that can't possibly be the heating system since I'm freezing cold. My breath fogs up in front of me again as I stand up, my body protesting the cold.

What the hell happened to the heat? This has to be some kind of joke... First the mishap with the reservation, and now this... Could this possibly be why the room was so cheap? I had thousands of points saved up for an extended vacation from my many years of traveling everywhere, and yes, I admit maybe this was too good to be true... and now it's starting to feel that way.

I step out of the room and into the hallway, moving as quietly as possible, not wanting to wake...*him.* The idea of bumping into Tom, who is sharing my dream villa, in the middle of the night when I'm already on edge from the cold doesn't sit well with me. I tiptoe down the stairs, shivering the whole way, and as I get closer to the living room, I hear the soft crackle of the fireplace.

Of course. Jesus, this might be a nightmare. If it weren't for the fact that my body is so cold, I would pinch myself to actually prove that I'm awake.

There he is. Sprawled out on the couch like it's his personal throne, one arm draped lazily over his eyes, the other hanging off the edge, his fingers lightly brushing the floor. He's shirtless. Again. I'm beginning to think he has an aversion to clothes, this man. Meanwhile, I'm freezing my butt off because he's turned the villa into a freaking igloo.

I stand there, teeth chattering, staring at him. He's got the fire blazing, but it's doing nothing to heat the rest of the place. The thermostat, which is faintly glowing on the wall, reads a solid sixty-four degrees. I don't understand Fahrenheit, but even I know that this has to be way too low. I feel my jaw tighten, and I resist the urge to stomp across the room and shove him off the couch. How can anyone be this inconsiderate? Is he trying to freeze me out?

I walk over to the wall and twist the dial to what I think is a reasonable temperature. The system clicks on immediately, sending a warm blast of air through the vent directly above me. I let out a slow breath, feeling a bit of relief as the warmth starts to circulate. But just as I'm about to head back upstairs, my new roommate stirs on the couch, groaning slightly. His arm drops from his eyes, and for a moment, he just stares up at the ceiling.

I freeze.

"What are you doing?" His voice is thick with sleep, rough around the edges in a way that makes me wish I had left ten seconds earlier. His eyes are still adjusting to the dim light, but there's a sharpness there now, like he's waking up to a problem he hasn't registered yet.

I cross my arms, the warmth of the heating system not doing enough to thaw my irritation. "What am *I* doing?" I snap, trying to keep my voice low but firm. "What are *you* doing, turning this place into a walk-in freezer? It's freezing upstairs."

His brow furrows, and he sits up slowly, rubbing his face with one hand. "I like it cold when I sleep," he mutters, as if that explains everything. "Helps me relax."

I roll my eyes, my arms still tight across my chest. "Then turn off the damn fireplace!"

He blinks at me, as if this entire conversation is just an inconvenience to him. His gaze flicks to the thermostat, where the temperature is gradually climbing. "Eighty degrees? Are you insane?" he spits out, although his voice is still low, still sleepy, but there's an undercurrent of something--sarcasm, maybe? Or indifference. Or maybe just the same annoyance he's had all day.

"I don't know! I don't understand Fahrenheit! I thought it was only *Americans* that used that." I huff, my frustration slowly starting to boil over. This is not the conversation I should be having and I don't owe him any explanations.

"Well," he lazed, sleepy and cozy. "I don't understand Celsius, because I'm *American*. And I didn't think it would affect you so much."

"Of course it affects me," I reply, my patience unraveling. "I'm not some Yeti monster. I actually like sleeping at a temperature where my blood doesn't freeze."

He watches me for a second, his eyes narrowing slightly. And then, to my complete and utter disbelief, a slow smile spreads across his face. "Of course you'll be cold if you're parading around the room half naked. Are you even wearing any clothes under that sweater?"

I stare at him, my mouth falling open. "Ugh! What the hell is wrong with you?"

"Oh, sweetheart," he drawls, standing slowly and walking in my direction. His gaze falls to my legs again, my toes curling inside my fuzzy socks at his perusal. I feel my blood start to boil, the cold long forgotten in the face of my rising frustration.

"What did you just call me?" My voice is sharp now, cutting through the quiet of the room.

He raises an eyebrow, clearly entertained, and walks past me to the dial, turning it down to somewhere in the low seventies. "I'll keep the room warm for you, sweetheart, don't worry."

I don't know whether to laugh or scream. The nerve of this man. "Don't call me that," I say through gritted teeth. "And don't act like you're doing me some grand favor. I shouldn't have to ask you to keep the place at a livable temperature."

He shrugs, completely unfazed by my anger. "Calm down. You don't have to get so worked up about it. Just tell me next time."

I stare at him, incredulous. "Tell you next time? I shouldn't have to—"

"Hey," he interrupts, his voice softening just a fraction. He's walking back to the couch now, his back on full display and his muscles so chiseled, even in the dim lighting. "It's not that big of a deal."

I blink, caught off guard by the dismissal in his tone. I cross my arms tighter, trying to hold on to my frustration, but the fight is draining out of me.

"Fine," I mutter, not really sure what else to say. The warmth in the room is starting to settle over me, and I suddenly feel exhausted. I glance back at him, shirtless on the couch, his hair a mess and his expression oddly serious. "That can't happen again."

I turn to leave, but as I reach the bottom of the stairs, I glance back. He's already lying down again, one arm thrown over his eyes, his body half lit by the glow of the fire. For some reason, I can't help but wonder what's behind that stoic exterior. What's hiding behind the annoyance and the careless attitude. There's more to him than just the irritation he causes me—something deeper, something I can't put my finger on.

"Goodnight," I say quietly, not really expecting a response.

He doesn't move, doesn't lift his arm from his face, but his voice drifts toward me, low and rough and strangely gentle. Maybe he's exhausted, too. "Goodnight."

5

CLARA

I WAKE up to soft light filtering through the sheer curtains. I must have forgotten to close the heavy blackout drapes again last night with all the confusion and the chaos and the freezer situation we had going on. The villa is silent, and the only sound I can hear coming from outside is a gentle thud in the distance, the same one I heard when I got off the shuttle bus that brought me from the airport.

I toss the covers off and swing my feet onto the hardwood floor, shivering a little as the cold bites at my toes. I must have taken off my cozy socks while I was asleep, because they lay discarded by the closet door. I put them on and shuffle to the bathroom, splashing some water on my face to shake off the remnants of sleep. I tossed and turned for a few hours after the heating fiasco until finally sleep caught up to me, and I'm tired, but there's a spark of energy because it's my first full day of vacation. A vacation I have been waiting for for so long, sometimes it feels a little surreal that I'm here.

Today, I'm going to stick to my plan. I'll have my breakfast alone, enjoy my morning, and pretend I'm not sharing this villa *con un idiota.*

The kitchen is quiet when I walk in, and I let out a breath of relief.

No Tom in sight. I can do this.

I'm halfway to the coffee maker when I hear the familiar sound of a chair scraping against the floor and I freeze. There he is, sitting at the dining room table, his back to me, hunched over a newspaper like a disgruntled old man. I blink, my earlier confidence evaporating as I realize he's already here, breaking our agreement. I really, *really* want to be by myself, *carajo.*

He glances up, his eyes meeting mine for a split second before he goes back to whatever he's doing with that newspaper. He's dressed in a different t-shirt and sweatpants than last night, his hair still damp from yet another shower. When did he even...? I shouldn't be thinking about his man taking a shower at all. I shouldn't care when he took a shower!

The sight of him is disarming—unexpectedly casual and almost...domestic. But there's nothing casual about the tension that fills the room, thick and uncomfortable.

"Morning," he says under his breath, his voice gruff, like he's trying so hard to keep it light but failing miserably.

"Good morning," I reply, forcing a smile that feels more like a grimace. I make a beeline for the coffee machine, trying to ignore the way my heart is hammering in my chest. This is fine. We're just two adults sharing a kitchen. No big deal.

I fumble with the buttons, trying to start the machine, but my hands feel clumsy, and I can't seem to get the water tank to fit right. I can feel his eyes on me, and the heat creeps up my neck.

"Is there a problem?" he asks, not unkindly, but still managing to sound like he's judging me.

"Nope, just...just fine," I mutter, finally getting the machine to cooperate. I can hear the faint hiss as the coffee starts brewing, and I grab a mug, clutching it like it's a lifeline.

I open the refrigerator door and, to my surprise, it's fully stocked. Three different kinds of milk, cold cuts, condiments. A few options of fruits and vegetables and eggs. There's a loaf of bread sitting on the counter by the toaster, the bag still closed.

"Um," I say out loud, trying to find the words in

my brain. But when I turn around, the man is gone and the villa is silent once again.

————

I spend the day wandering through town, taking my time with every little shop and café. The snow is powdery and perfect, blanketing everything in a crisp bright white, and I feel a strange kind of giddiness watching kids build snowmen and couples skate on the frozen rink in the center of the mountain village. I've never felt anything like this—this crisp cold, this brightness. It's invigorating, and for a few hours, I manage to forget about the mess back at the villa and back home.

By the time I return, I'm exhausted and cold, in desperate need of a shower to warm me up, and the thought of seeing Tom again has my nerves frayed. The sun is setting, casting a golden light over the snowy landscape, and when I step inside, I can already feel the shift in the air. He is sprawled on the sofa, flipping through the TV channels with the remote. One of his legs is stretched long on the cushions, the other is bent, foot planted on the floor.

He glances up as I close the door, and I can see the weariness in his eyes.

"Rough day?" I ask, kicking off my boots near the door. They land with a wet thud, leaving a trail of slushy snow on the floor. I shrug out of my coat, suddenly feeling too warm, even with the chill that's clung to me since I left the café.

My roommate sets the remote down, rubbing his shoulder absently like it aches. "You could say that." His voice is lower than usual, tired, like he's been carrying more than just ski gear on his shoulders. And it's there again, that faraway look, that says everything but nothing at the same time. I shouldn't want to decipher it.

I hesitate, torn between wanting to retreat to the shower and this unexpected urge to linger just a little longer, to know more. "What happened?" I end up blurting, and a blush starts creeping up my neck and into my cheeks. I've never been more grateful for dim lighting in my life.

He sighs, leaning back against the sofa. "Nothing." He runs a hand through his hair, and for the first time, I notice the faint traces of exhaustion etched in his features, lines that weren't visible in the sharpness and heat of our previous encounters.

I look at him, studying his face for a second longer than I intend.

"Binding broke on my left ski. Halfway down a slope. Had to hike back up in the snow with one good ski and a whole lot of bad luck."

"I did not understand a single word of what you just said but it sounds... awful?" I move closer, still keeping a polite distance but suddenly aware of how small the villa feels with the two of us in it. "I don't ski, but even I know that sounds miserable."

He chuckles, a sound so brief it's almost easy to miss. "Yeah, it wasn't my finest moment. This trip has been one thing after the other, I swear." His face softens for just a second, and I catch a glimpse of something more vulnerable beneath the layers of irritation and distance. It's unexpected, this little crack in his armor.

"Yeah, but maybe look at the bright side," I say, straightening and walking towards the stairs. "It's led you to me."

There's a flicker of a smile, not warm but not harsh either. I don't know what I'm doing. I don't know *why* I'm doing it. I shouldn't be tempting fate, but I can't help but smile back. I shift, suddenly feeling out of place in my own villa. Or at least, what should be mine. "That's why you're such an asshole, then?" I tease lightly, trying to pull him back from wherever his mind has wandered.

He glances at me, and for the first time, his smile reaches his eyes, if only just. "I'm not that big of an asshole. I just happen to not like blonde, blue-eyed intruders in my own hotel room."

I let out an incredulous laugh, the sound escaping before I can stop it. "Oh, is that what we're calling it now? Because I distinctly remember being here first. And I probably can get you some receipts."

He snorts and his gaze finds my lips. It catches me off guard, and I feel my cheeks heat. Is he...flirting? No, probably not. But still, there's something different here, something warmer that throws me off balance. I latch on to it, curious despite myself. "Why didn't you just... I don't know, yell at me or something? You seemed more annoyed than surprised."

He shrugs, leaning back and crossing his arms. "I've been living out of hotels and rental places for months. Mistakes happen. I figured you'd freak out and leave. But you didn't. You stayed. That was... unexpected."

The admission lands heavier than I anticipate, and I find myself holding his gaze a second too long before glancing away and looking into the fireplace. *Unexpected.* Yeah, he has no idea.

"Well, I don't scare easily." I meet his gaze, and for the first time, it feels like we're on even ground. "And I was promised a solo adventure. Not an adventure with the prickliest man in town."

His smile lingers, softer now, and I see a flicker of understanding there, an unspoken acknowledgement of our shared annoyances. It's not friendship, not by a long shot, but it's something.

"I'm not usually like this," he says, almost to himself. "Just... been a long year."

"It's only February," I say with a laugh. "But I get it." I sink into the armchair opposite him, feeling the weight of my own few years settle on my shoulders. "I'm not usually this snippy either. But this year's been... well, weird."

Tom raises an eyebrow, intrigued. "Weird how?"

I hesitate, but his question doesn't feel invasive, just curious. Like a little deeper small talk you would have with your local barista. "I had this plan, you know? Go on a trip, disconnect, figure things out. I've been running on autopilot for a while—work, relationships, just...life. Thought I'd take a break and maybe find whatever it is I've been missing." I glance at him, suddenly self-conscious. "Not that it's working out exactly how I planned."

He nods, absorbing my words, and for a moment, the tension between us dissolves, replaced by something quieter, more understanding. "Sometimes you just need to get away from it all, even if it's just to figure out what the hell you're doing. The forest for the trees and whatnot."

I smile, the warmth in his tone surprising me, yet again. It's the most real moment we've shared since this whole mess started, and I feel a small flicker of something that wasn't there before—maybe it's understanding, or maybe it's just relief that he's not the one-dimensional jerk I'd painted him as.

"Well," I say, pushing up from the chair, "at least

we've got a good view while we figure it out." I nod toward the window, where the mountains are bathed in the last light of day, snow glistening like a scene from a fairytale.

He follows my gaze, his eyes softening at the sight. "Yeah," he agrees, his voice quiet. "Could be worse."

6

TOM

THIS ENTIRE TRIP has been one misstep after another, and my body's still sore from that binding mishap on the slopes yesterday. I make my way over to the resort's spa, slipping past the bustling lobby, and manage to book a massage with surprisingly little hassle. I'm assuming the majority of the guests spend their days skiing and show up for their massages after the lifts are closed, and the chances of the agenda being completely booked at midday are low.

Ten minutes later, I'm wrapped in a plush red robe and escorted into the dim, eucalyptus-scented waiting room. A small tabletop water feature sits in the corner, the only sound coming from the liquid hitting the flat stones at the bottom. I settle back on the chair, exhaling a long breath, trying to let the stress slip away.

A door opens slowly, and I assume it's my massage therapist until I hear a familiar sigh—a sigh that's been directed at me more than a handful of times in the past few days. I glance over, only to find Clara standing there in the same red robe I'm wearing, her face reflecting the same shock I feel.

She narrows her eyes at me. "What are you doing here?"

"Funny," I say, sitting up straighter. "I was just about to ask you the same thing."

She lets out an exasperated laugh. "You know—"

Before she can retort, a cheerful spa attendant steps in, looking back and forth between us with a grin that tells me she's fully bought into whatever Valentine's Day marketing scheme the resort has been pushing.

"Welcome!" she chirps, so similar to that front desk woman that I actually start doubting if they're not the same person. "Mr. and Mrs. Hall," she says, looking between us.

Clara and I both sputter at the same time.

"No, no—"

"We're not—" I try to say.

The spa attendant just laughs and winks at me. "Oh, sorry! We just go by what's in the system. Apologies for that." There's a big smile on her face and she looks at me, like I'm hiding something and we are complicit in the same secret. "If you follow me, I'll take you to your room." She beams as though she's announced a free vacation.

Clara's cheeks flush, her jaw tightening as she looks at me, clearly frustrated. "There must be some mistake," she says, indignation all over her face. I feel the same way, because these things can't keep happening to us. "I just came here for a massage."

I nod, my irritation matching her. "Same here. Can we just... fix this?"

The attendant looks between us, the brightness in her eyes dimming just a little. "I'm afraid we're fully booked today. We can cancel your appointment, of course, but unfortunately, we wouldn't be able to fit you both in separately until sometime next week."

Clara lets out a long breath, throwing a look my way, clearly debating whether to put up with yet *another* mistake or lose her massage slot altogether.

She glances at me and mutters, "Fine. Whatever. Let's just do this."

I stifle a groan. I don't need more proximity to this woman. This is the very last thing I expected for what I thought would be a relaxing day, but I'm not about to lose my only chance to ease this muscle tension. I nod to the attendant. "Let's get it over with, then."

She leads us down a short hallway, past a string of softly lit rooms, until we arrive at a private suite with two massage tables set side by side. There's a large, floor-to-ceiling window at the back, and two small chairs facing it. The room is filled with soft music and the faint scent of lavender. And lit candles. Everywhere. On every surface, on the floor, around the massage tables. It's unreal and completely unnecessary.

Clara and I eye each other, both of us clearly less than thrilled with the setup.

The attendant hands each of us a glass of a sparkling beverage that looks suspiciously like wine and says with another conspiratorial grin, "Your therapists will be right in. Just get comfortable, and enjoy your experience together." With a small wave, she disappears out the door, and Clara sighs. The most dramatic one yet.

"This," she mutters, making her way to the chairs facing the window, her steps cautious to avoid any flames, I assume, "is exactly the kind of nonsense I wanted to avoid."

"Believe me," I say, following her but stopping short and placing my drink on a small side table. "I'd rather be getting my own massage than sharing this with someone who thinks my entire existence is a nuisance," I shoot back, not exactly feeling the warm and fuzzies this setup is trying to do either.

She shrugs and sits down, closing her eyes and

taking a deep breath. "Can't help it if the truth's hard to hear."

I roll my eyes and take off my robe, hanging it on the hook on the wall closest to one of the massage tables. There's silence for a moment as I settle, face down, covering myself with the warm blanket and trying to relax despite the awkwardness hovering in the room like a big, fat elephant.

"Turn around," she says, as if she can't tell I'm facing down with my head on the headrest and my eyes closed, trying to zone out and ignore the world around me. "Don't look."

I snort. "Yeah okay."

"You're such an asshole, you know—"

The massage therapists choose that moment to enter, their calm tones and gentle introductions at least partially distracting me from the fact that I'm stuck in a couple's massage with a very tense woman next to me. This resort is huge, with plenty of indoor and outdoor activities to entertain us, and we seem to end up in the same space consistently.

But soon enough, the therapist's hands start working out the tension in my shoulders, and I finally feel a bit of the stress melting away. If I weren't so on edge already, I would have used this time to think about my next steps. I had an enlightening conversation with my business partner last week, where we discussed the future of our business and our partnership, and I finally brought up some things I was not comfortable with and some other things I wanted to try instead of the intense business of breeding and growing elite horses.

Just as I'm starting to relax, Clara speaks, her voice low. "Are you enjoying this?"

"Enjoying what?" I ask, keeping my tone light. "This romantic, cozy bonding moment with my roommate? It's the highlight of my trip, to be honest."

"Ugh," she groans, but there's a hint of amusement under her frustration. "Do you think they think we're together and maybe you are asking me to marry you?"

"What?" I lift my head and snap my eyes in her direction, but she's still facing down, her arms hanging by her head and her fingers dancing on the floor, one of them playing with a rose petal.

She lets out a sigh, and I catch a glimpse of her face turning toward me, but the moment she notices I'm looking she shifts back, resting it on the headpiece and mumbling something I quite don't understand.

I turn my face back down, smirking into the headrest. She may have turned away quickly, but I caught the faint blush that colored her cheeks. For a woman who seems to hate my guts, Clara sure has a lot to say.

"Are you... flattered?" I ask, keeping my voice light. "Because it sounds like you're putting a lot of thought into this fake proposal scenario."

"Oh, please." She scoffs, but her tone is playful,

just like the glimpse I got of her last night. "I'm simply amused by how easily you fit into every Valentine's cliché this resort has cooked up. It's like you were destined to play the brooding, reluctant male main character."

"Brooding?" I chuckle. "I didn't realize you'd been studying me so closely, sweetheart. Guess I'm flattered, then," I drawl.

"In your dreams, Thomas," she says, but I can hear the hint of a smile in her voice. "The whole setup's ridiculous, that's all. Rose petals, candles, a couple's massage room... Seriously, what's next? Chocolates on our pillows? 'Will you marry me?' written with these same rose petals on the bed back in the room?"

"Probably," I mumble, half to myself. "This place seems determined to play matchmaker."

Clara laughs, and for the first time, it sounds genuine, free from the usual bite. It's a sound that tugs at something in my chest I'd rather ignore. The room falls into a peaceful silence, and for a moment, I let myself sink into the rhythm of the massage, the soft background music, and the quiet.

It's... almost nice.

Almost.

The massage therapists eventually step out, leaving us alone in the room again. I roll onto my side, pulling the blanket with me and glancing over at Clara, who is doing the same.

"Well," she says, lifting her chin with a mock formality. "It's been... tolerable."

"Glad I could live up to the bare minimum," I shoot back, smirking.

She stands, gathering her robe and slipping it back on, cinching the belt tightly. "For what it's worth," she says, glancing at me from beneath her lashes, "I would have said no if you actually proposed. I mean, what kind of monster proposes at a spa of all places?"

I pause, the words hanging between us as warmth spreads through my body and a loud, long burst of laughter erupts in my chest. She's smiling and her blue eyes are shining, but she's quick to tamp her smile down. I clear my throat, fighting to keep my expression neutral. "I'll take that as a compliment, I guess?"

"Don't," she says with a shrug, but her lips quirk up at the edges. "It was just an observation."

She turns to leave, pausing only briefly to flash me one last look—one that, for the first time, doesn't carry her usual edge of irritation.

7

CLARA

THE KITCHEN IS WARM, bathed in the soft morning light that filters through the back windows, making everything feel golden and quiet. I'm still not used to waking up in this villa, half expecting the space to feel cold and unfamiliar, but it's starting to grow on me, even with Tom around. *Especially with Tom around*, I realize, as I catch sight of him by the coffee machine, already making a fresh cup.

"Morning," he says, glancing up. His brown eyes are set intently on me, studying my face with *a lot* of attention to detail. And there's no gruffness in his voice today, just an easy familiarity that slowly seeped into this shared villa and settled between us. He hands me a mug without me even asking, and it's such a simple thing, but it catches me off guard.

"Morning," I reply, wrapping my hands around the warm ceramic. "Thanks."

He nods, and we stand there for a moment, just sipping our coffee. It's almost...comfortable, this quiet, shared routine we've stumbled into. I don't think I've been this comfortable since Santiago, and we all know how that ended, so this needs to be shut down, immediately. As soon as I'm done with my coffee, I'm walking away and staying away for the whole day.

I pour some milk into my mug, watching the swirl of colors meld together, and for a second, I forget the awkwardness that hung between us just a few days ago.

"I'm going to make some eggs," Tom says, breaking the silence. He's already cracking them into a pan, moving around the kitchen with an ease I didn't expect. "Want some?"

I tilt my head to the side, focusing on what his hands are doing. "That's such an American thing, having eggs at breakfast. I don't think I've ever had them for breakfast before."

He blinks, a little surprised and confused. "Then what do you eat for breakfast?"

"Toast? I don't know, something that is not eggs. Pastries. Fruit?"

"Toast with what? Just toast?"

"Jam?" I reply, but it comes out as a question almost. "Why are you looking at me like that?"

"Like what?" he says, turning back to the eggs in question and mixing them with a wooden spoon. "I'm not looking at you."

Tom's confusion is almost endearing, and I can't help but laugh at the way he looks at me, like I've just told him I don't eat breakfast at all. There's something about his earnestness that catches me off guard, a softness that has been showing up more and more as the days go by.

"Jam and toast," I repeat, still amused. "It's not that weird."

Tom glances at me, his brow furrowed in a way that is half skeptical, half curious. "It's a little weird. Bland, maybe?" he says, shaking his head as he continues to stir the eggs. "I mean, you're missing out on the best part of breakfast. Eggs are—"

"Are what?" I interrupt, leaning against the counter and watching him with a grin. "A delicacy? A must-have? The peak of American cuisine?"

He smirks, shrugging one shoulder as he adds a pinch of salt to the pan. "Pretty much. Eggs are, like, the backbone of breakfast. Protein, Clara. It's what gets you through the day."

I laugh, genuinely amused by his seriousness.

"Okay, but explain to me how jam on toast doesn't do the same. It's fruit. And bread. Carbs and... whatever jam is made of. It's fine."

Tom turns off the stove and slides the scrambled eggs onto two plates, handing me one. "Here. Consider this your first American breakfast experience." He's teasing, I know it, but there's a flicker of something else in his eyes—maybe pride or just the simple pleasure of sharing something familiar with someone else.

I take the plate, the eggs steaming and looking fluffier than I expected. "Fine," I say, taking a bite, and I have to admit, they're pretty good. Simple, comforting in a way I didn't think they'd be. "Not bad. I'll give that to you."

He grins, leaning against the island next to me, his shoulder brushing mine in a way that feels accidental and deliberate all at once. "See? Stick with me, and I'll have you eating pancakes and bacon by the end of the week."

"Pancakes? Now you're pushing it," I say, but I can't help the smile that tugs at my lips. There's something about this back-and-forth, this light teasing, that feels effortless, like slipping into a rhythm I didn't know we could have.

———

After breakfast, Tom and I go our separate ways, but we keep crossing paths like it's inevitable. I see him at the ski rental shop, testing out something that I assume are bindings, his expression focused and serious. We exchange a quick nod, the kind that feels more like a silent conversation. Later, at the little café by the ice skating rink, he's at the counter ordering a coffee, and I wave from my table. It's small moments, fleeting but easy, like the universe keeps nudging us together.

By early afternoon, I find myself at the Valentine's Day craft fair, my breath visible in the crisp air, surrounded by the sounds of festive music and the hum of happy chatter. Booths line the cobblestone path that looks completely out of place in such a master-planned town, like maybe the only reason why this path is here is for this exact reason. Each vendor offers something different—handmade crafts, hot mulled wine, natural wreaths adorned with Valentine's Day ornaments. It's charming in a way that's almost overwhelming, and I let myself get lost in the sights and smells, moving from one stall to the next.

I spot Tom by a stand that sells carved wooden animals, his attention fixed on a small horse. He turns it over in his hands, examining the intricate details, and there's a softness in his expression that I haven't seen before. I hesitate, wondering if I should interrupt, but then he looks up and catches me watching.

"See something you like?" I ask, walking up to him, my hands stuffed in my pockets.

He makes a gesture with his hand and mouths "one minute," and that's when I notice he is on the phone.

I step back, pretending to browse the neighboring stall, but I can't help myself—I'm listening. Tom's voice is softer than what I've ever heard, almost tender, and it catches me off guard.

"Hey, honey," he says, and my heart drops to my stomach. There's an intimacy in the way he says it, a kind of warmth that I've never heard from him before. I shift my focus to a display of ceramic mugs, running my fingers along the rim of one, trying to ground myself, but my mind is spinning.

Tom's voice carries over the noise of the market, low and filled with quiet affection. "I miss you, too. It's not the same here without you." His words are so gentle, so personal, and suddenly, I feel like I'm intruding on something I have no business hearing.

I turn the mug over in my hand, staring at the intricate pattern painted on its surface, but my thoughts are miles away. Who is she? His girlfriend? His wife? My chest tightens, and I feel a ridiculous pang of jealousy that I have no right to feel. Tom and I are practically strangers; we've only just started tolerating each other's presence. But hearing him talk like this, knowing there's someone else he's connected to —it stings more than it should.

"I wish I could be there," Tom continues, his voice dipping lower, as if he's trying to keep this moment just between them. "I love you, too."

I set the mug down a little too forcefully, my pulse quickening. This isn't what I signed up for. I didn't come here to feel like some outsider looking in on a relationship I can't ever be part of. I'm here to *find myself.* Not a freaking man.

I take a few steps back, wanting to put distance between us, between whatever this strange, sinking feeling is.

I glance back at Tom just as he's hanging up, slipping his phone into his pocket. He turns to me, and there's that softness still lingering in his expression, like he's carrying the weight of that conversation with him.

"Sorry about that," he says, his voice back to its usual tone, but there's a lingering warmth there, something that hasn't faded away. "Didn't mean to make you wait."

I force a smile, hoping it doesn't look as strained as it feels. "No worries. Everything okay?"

"Yeah," he says, nodding, but he doesn't elaborate. He's already moved on, picking up the little horse again and turning it over in his hands. But I can't shake the heavy feeling, the jealousy curling in my chest like a hot, uncomfortable knot. I've been here before—getting too close to someone, only to find out they're already tangled up with someone else. And it's exactly what I need to get away from right now.

We walk through the rest of the market together, but my mind is only half present, caught between our earlier easy banter and the reality of what I overheard. I try to laugh at his jokes, to smile at the right moments, but everything feels a little off-kilter now, like I'm pretending to be okay when I'm not. I keep wondering about the person on the other end of his call, about who she is to him, and why it bothers me so much.

I mean, I partially know why it bothers me so much... Because in a weird, fucked up turn of events, I felt like the other woman for years, even though he didn't cheat on me at all. And a few months ago, Santiago married someone else, when it had been clear for years, at least to me, that I was going to be the person to marry him.

As the sun starts to set, the resort begins setting up for the evening's lights display. The sky is streaked with shades of pink and orange, and couples and families are gathering near the bonfire, their faces lit up with the warm glow of anticipation. I find a spot on a bench facing the mountain, and Tom follows behind, sitting down on the other end, our bodies completely separated by a few of the hotel-provided blankets.

"What are we watching?" he asks, his gaze set on the face of the mountain where the main chair lift operates.

"It's the Valentine's Day torchlight parade. The receptionist called this morning to let me know it was happening."

At that exact second, the crowd gasps as the first skier appears at the top of the run, a red flare in one hand, moving from side to side in tandem with the music. A few more follow, and it's a matter of seconds until the whole mountain is covered in red. An accurate choreographed display of lights and movement, skiers weaving down the slope in perfect unison, their flares casting an eerie, beautiful glow against the snow. It's mesmerizing, like watching a river of fire flow down the mountainside.

"Wow," I say, my voice barely louder than a whisper, not wanting to disturb the peaceful atmosphere.

He nods, his eyes still fixed on the mountain. "Yeah, it's..." He clears his throat. "It's something else."

The last skier reaches the base and the crowd erupts in applause, cheers echoing through the crisp evening air. I feel a sudden rush of cold as the sun finally dips behind the peaks, and I pull a blanket tight around my shoulders, trying to hold on to the fleeting warmth.

Tom notices, his gaze flicking to me for a moment. Without saying a word, he reaches over, pulling his side of the blanket towards me, closing the gap between us. Our arms brush as he adjusts the fabric, and I feel a jolt of electricity shoot through me. It's just a blanket, just a simple, practical gesture, but the proximity, the unexpected contact, sends my heart racing.

"Here," he says, his voice softer now, almost gentle. "You're freezing."

I nod, swallowing hard as I let the blanket settle over both of us, our bodies now closer than they've ever been all week. The fabric is warm, but his presence is warmer, and I'm suddenly hyper-aware of every tiny movement—his shoulder brushing mine, his knee pressing lightly against my thigh. It's not much, but it's enough to set every nerve in my body on edge.

I try to focus on the fireworks starting in the distance, the sky erupting into bursts of red and white, but all I can think about is the heat radiating from Tom, the way his arm lingers just a little too long against mine. There's an intimacy in it that catches me off guard, something that feels both innocent and charged, like we're toeing the line between strangers and something more.

Tom shifts slightly, and his leg brushes against mine, sending another spark skittering through my veins. I can't tell if it's intentional or just the natural result of sharing a small space, but it doesn't matter.

It's enough to make me catch my breath, my mind reeling with the sudden, overwhelming awareness of him.

I turn to say something—anything to break this tension—but the words die on my lips when I see the fire in his eyes. There's something there, something urgent and heavy, and it's the kind of look that makes my stomach flip in a way I haven't felt in a long time.

"Ready to leave?" he whispers in my ear, his breath warm and sweet.

The fireworks explode in a series of rapid bursts, the noise drowning out everything but the thudding of my heart. I should move, get up and put some distance between us, walk back to the villa and lock myself in my bedroom until it's time to leave this mountain. But I can't bring myself to do it. Not when the air between us feels so charged, so full of possibility.

"Yep," I say as I get up hastily from the bench. I stumble as I stand, my foot catching on the edge of the blanket, and before I know it, I'm off balance, pitching forward. The world tilts, and for a split second, all I see is the blur of the ground rushing up to meet me. But then, Tom's arm is around my waist, strong and steady, pulling me back before I can fall completely.

"Whoa, easy," he whispers, his voice low and calming as he steadies me, his hands gripping either side of my body just a little too tightly, fingers pressing into my skin. The heat of his touch sends a shiver down my spine, and I'm suddenly hyper-aware of the firmness of his chest, the way his fingers linger as if reluctant to let go.

His touch is electric, grounding and overwhelming all at once, and my heart is racing, not just from the near fall but from the way his presence wraps around me, warm and consuming.

"I— Uh, I'm just gonna..." I mumble, gesturing vaguely towards the villa in the distance, my mind spinning in a dozen different directions. The only thing I can hear is the beat of my heart, a reminder that this is wrong, that Tom's not mine to think about like this. But my body isn't listening; it's already memorizing the warmth of his touch, the way his fingers feel against my skin.

"Clara, sweetheart," he says softly, and the sound of my name on his lips makes something flutter deep in my chest. It's tender, the way he says it, like he's asking me to stay, to not run away from whatever just sparked between us.

The loud applause breaks me from my panic.

"I'm just... I need to head back," I stammer, backing away, my eyes darting everywhere but at him. "Long day, you know?"

Tom watches me, his expression unreadable, and for a second, I think he might stop me, that he might say something to acknowledge whatever just happened between us. But he doesn't. He just nods, his gaze following me as I fumble with the blankets and make my escape.

I hurry back to the villa and once inside, I slam the door to my room, leaning against it as I catch my breath, my heart still fluttering in my chest. I'm trying to process it all—the warmth of his touch, the way he looked at me like I was the only person in the world—it's too much.

But it's there. And it's undeniable.

8

TOM

I'VE BEEN STARING at the coffee pot for what feels like an eternity, trying to shake off the tension from last night. There's a heaviness in my chest that wasn't there before, a lingering charge that refuses to let me go.

Clara hasn't come out of her room yet, and I'm half relieved, half disappointed. I don't know what I'm supposed to say to her after the way we left things. That moment sitting on the bench watching whatever that parade was, the way her body felt pressed against mine—it's been on a loop in my head since I got back. The softness of her skin, the hitch in her breath when I caught her before she fell. I haven't been able to stop thinking about it, and it's messing with my head.

The villa feels too quiet, the kind of quiet that only

highlights how alone I've been, how much I've been missing. It's a stark contrast to the noise of my usual life—press conferences, crowds, the constant hum of expectation. But here, it's just me and my thoughts, and lately, those thoughts have been wrapped around the gorgeous blonde more than I care to admit.

I hear her door open, the soft click of it pulling me out of my head. Clara steps down the stairs and into the kitchen, her hair slightly tousled, wearing an over-sized sweater that looks like it's swallowing her whole. She pauses when she sees me and clears her throat. "Hi," she says, her voice tentative, as if she's testing the waters.

"Hi," I reply, trying to keep my tone light and casual, like nothing's changed. But it has. I can feel it in the way she's avoiding my gaze, her focus on the coffee pot instead of me.

We stand there in silence, tension hanging heavy in the air between us. I should say something, make a joke, anything to break this awkwardness, but my mouth feels like it's filled with lead. She makes herself a cup of coffee, her movements slow, deliberate, and for a moment, it's like we're strangers all over again.

"I'm going to—"

"About last night—"

We both speak up at the same time, but I shut my mouth immediately, because it was clearly the last thing Clara wanted to hear. She recoils, walking backwards with her mug clutched against her chest. "I'm taking a ski lesson today. Gotta run."

I watch her retreat, her footsteps quick and purposeful as she moves towards the stairs, but there's a slight tremble in her hand that gives her away. Clara is not as put together as she's pretending to be, and that flicker of vulnerability—the one she's trying so hard to hide—only makes my chest tighten more.

"Clara, wait—" I start, but she's already in her room, the sound of the door closing echoing through the villa. The silence that follows is deafening, the kind that digs in deep and won't let go. I'm left standing there, my coffee untouched, staring at the space where she'd been just moments before, her scent still lingering in the air—something floral and soft, like jasmine.

I take a long breath, running a hand through my hair, trying to pull myself together. This was supposed to be simple. Just a few days away from work, a chance to clear my head, spend quality time with my daughter and figure out what the hell I'm doing with my life. But now, it feels like everything's been flipped on its head, and it's all because of her. Clara, with her bright eyes and easy laugh, her habit of walking into a room and lighting it up without even trying.

I head to the living room, slumping onto the couch, the weight of it all pressing down on me. It's ridiculous how quickly this got complicated, how fast she's gotten under my skin. I can't remember the last time I felt this way—like I was right on the edge of something I couldn't quite control, something that could either be the best or the worst thing to happen to me.

After what feels like hours, I grab my jacket and head outside. I need the cold air, the sting of winter biting at my skin, something to jolt me out of this mess in my head. All my attention should be on my daughter or my career path, but I can't even manage a simple call with her without turning my head and looking for Clara everywhere.

The snow crunches under my boots as I make my way down the trail towards the lobby. The sky is gray and heavy, the kind that promises more snow, and for once, the idea of getting lost in it doesn't seem so bad.

I stand out on the back patio for a bit, scrolling through my work emails and endless messages, catching up on the few photos Erin sent me of their staycation in the snow. It seems ironic, that all I wanted was to take some time with my daughter and bring her to the snow and, unintentionally, my ex-wife got to do that.

And that pisses me off even more, because it was supposed to be my plan. It was my idea.

I push off the railing and start walking toward the bunny slope, where a group of adults are going up the magic carpet, the slow, outdoor conveyor that takes them up the hill, and then down the beginner run trying to grasp the basics of skiing. And it's unmistakable—Clara's hair flapping in the wind behind her, an exhilarated yell as she makes her way down the tiny hill.

"You're doing great," I call out, my voice light, trying to keep it casual. She glances over, surprised to see me standing there, but she doesn't say anything. Her skis keep sliding in my direction and panic covers her face.

"Tom," she starts, but she's cut off as her ski slips out from under her, sending her stumbling forward. I reach out instinctively, catching her around the waist before she can hit the ground. It's a familiar feeling now, the way her body fits against mine, the warmth of her even through the layers of winter gear.

We're close again, too close, and it's like everything else falls away—the resort, the snow, the lingering voices of the other skiers. It's just her, pressed up against me, her breath hitching as she steadies herself.

"You okay?" I ask, my voice rougher than I intend.

She nods, but she doesn't pull away immediately, her hands lingering on my arms as if she's not ready to let go. "Yeah. I'm just... Sorry."

Our eyes meet, and there's that spark again, that magnetic pull that's been there since the first time we met, simmering under the surface. I don't know what to say, don't know how to navigate this without making things worse, but the silence between us is charged, crackling with everything we're not saying.

"Clara," I start, my grip on her waist tightening just slightly, but she slides back, putting space between us. Her movements are awkward and almost like a baby giraffe with her skis on, and it takes her a while to finally turn away from me.

"I should—" she stammers, glancing back between her instructor and me. The group is all looking in our direction, waiting for her to join them. "I should get back."

I step back, my hands dropping to my sides as she straightens, brushing something invisible from her jacket. She doesn't look at me right away, instead focusing on adjusting her skis and avoiding the gaze of the instructor waiting a few yards away.

"Thanks for catching me," she mutters, her voice barely audible over the low hum of skiers slowly gliding by. There's a group of tiny children giggling close by, and their laughter and shrieks of amusement pierce the air.

"Anytime," I reply, shrugging like it's no big deal. But it feels bigger than I want it to. The accidental touches, the way her eyes linger just a little too long, the strange pull that's been building between us—it's all starting to crack through the walls I've put up.

Since my marriage was over, and my focus was on my career and providing for my daughter.

Clara finally meets my gaze, her eyes sharp but softened by something I can't identify. "Don't get used to it," she says, the corners of her mouth turning up ever so slightly. "I'm not planning on falling again."

"Sure you aren't," I reply, smirking. "But just in case, I'll be around."

She rolls her eyes, but there's a glint in them, a flicker of something playful, and for a moment, it feels like we're teetering on the edge of something new. The instructor calls her over, breaking the moment, and she takes a small, shaky breath before nodding to him.

"See you later," she says, her voice steady again, as if regaining her footing. She pushes off, turning her focus back to the hill, leaving me standing there with a strange sense of satisfaction—and the realization that maybe, just maybe, I wouldn't mind if she needed another hand to hold.

9

CLARA

I DISAPPEAR into my room without a word, feeling the sting of cold mountain air still clinging to my skin, my cheeks flushed from the wind and whatever just happened with Tom on the slope. My body feels jittery, like it does when I've had too much coffee before work. The way his hands steadied me, the feel of his chest against mine, the heat of his touch lingering longer than it should. I can't shake it off, can't pretend that my heart didn't skip a beat when I looked up and saw him standing there, watching me like I was the only thing in his line of sight.

I flop on my bed, staring at the ceiling, and try to push the thoughts away. It's just attraction, I tell myself. Just the rush of being in close quarters with a handsome man, who, despite everything and the quirky circumstances, makes me feel seen. It doesn't mean anything. It can't mean anything.

I stand on a groan and head for the shower, stripping off my clothes and stepping under the hot spray. The water scalds my skin at first, but I welcome it, letting the heat seep into my bones, washing away the cold and the tension that's been coiled tight in my chest since last night.

I close my eyes, leaning my forehead against the cool tiles, and try to focus on the steady rhythm of the water. But all I can see is Tom's face, the way his eyes darkened when he caught me for a second time, the hint of something in his expression that I can't place. Something that makes me feel like I'm just not imagining this pull between us.

When I finally step out, my skin feels raw and new, and I wrap myself in a towel, padding quietly back to my room. I put on the first comfortable thing I can find —leggings and another oversized sweater, soft and warm, like armor against whatever's happening outside this room. I take a moment, staring at my reflection in the mirror, trying to make sense of the girl looking back at me.

I've been here before, haven't I? Getting too close, feeling too much, reading into things that aren't meant for me. The thought of Tom's voice on the phone from the other day flits through my mind—

honey—and the way he said it, so intimate, so familiar. It's the reminder I need to put some distance between us, to keep my guard up because I know how this story ends.

But the knot in my stomach tells me it's already too late for that.

I walk back out to the kitchen, my hair still damp and curling at the ends, and find Tom leaning against the island, staring at the coffee machine like it holds all the answers of the universe. He looks up when he hears me coming, his eyes scanning me intently, sending a shiver down my spine.

"Hello," I say, my voice soft, tentative, like we're on the edge of something fragile.

"Hey," he replies, setting his mug down. He's wearing a plain t-shirt and jeans, casual but effortless, and I can't help but notice how his shoulders fill out the fabric, how he's always just...there. Solid and steady, in a way that feels like a challenge to my resolve.

There's a moment where neither of us moves, where we're just standing there, watching each other, the silence between us thick with unspoken words. I should say something, anything, to break this tension, but my brain is moving too fast, tripping over itself trying to keep up with my heart.

"About earlier," I start, but the words catch in my throat. I don't know how to explain what I'm feeling, don't know how to make sense of it when I'm not even sure myself. "I didn't mean to—"

"You didn't do anything," he cuts in, his voice gentle, but there's an edge to it, like he's fighting something back. "I'm the one who—"

We both stop, our words colliding and falling apart, and for a second, it's like we're back on that bench last night, too close and too afraid to do anything about it. I can feel the pull between us, magnetic and undeniable, and it's like the room has shrunk around us, drawing us in.

I take a step closer, and he doesn't move, his eyes fixed on mine, and I can see the conflict there—the push and pull of whatever this is, whatever we're dancing around. My heart is pounding so loud I'm sure he can hear it, and every nerve in my body is screaming at me to stop, to turn around and walk away. He's taken. His heart belongs to someone else, and I shouldn't be doing this at all. Probably shouldn't even be looking in his direction.

But I don't stop.

I take another step, closing the space between us, and I can feel the heat of him, the way his breath hitches as I reach up, my fingers brushing lightly against his jaw. It's a tentative touch, testing the waters, and when he doesn't pull away, I let my hand linger, tracing the line of his cheekbone.

"Tom," I whisper, my voice barely audible, and it's like the last barrier between us shatters.

He moves so fast I barely register it, his hands cupping my face as he leans in, his lips finding mine with a hunger that steals my breath.

The kiss is soft at first, hesitant, like we're both afraid to push too far, but it doesn't take long for it to deepen, for the slow burn that's been building between us to ignite. His lips are warm and firm, and he kisses me like he's been wanting for this, like he's been holding back for so long and he's finally letting go.

I gasp against his mouth, my hands tangling through his hair as I pull him closer, and he responds in kind, his grip tightening on my waist. There's nothing tentative about this now—it's urgent and desperate, a clash of need and want that's been simmering under the surface for days. I can feel his heartbeat against my chest, frantic and matching mine, and I lose myself in the feel of him, the taste of him.

When we finally break apart, we're both breathless, staring at each other with wide eyes, and I can see the same mix of confusion and exhilaration mirrored in his expression. His thumb brushes against my cheek, a lingering touch that sends a fresh wave of heat through me.

"We shouldn't have—" I begin, my voice unsteady,

but the truth is, I don't know how to finish that sentence. I don't want to finish it.

"Yeah," he says, his forehead resting against mine, his breath warm against my skin. "But I'm not sorry."

I close my eyes, letting his words sink in, and for a moment, I forget about everything else—the doubt, the uncertainty, the voice in my head telling me to back away. It's just us, here in this villa, caught in a moment that feels both reckless and right.

But reality creeps in, and I pull back, just enough to see the conflict in his eyes, the same one that's swirling in my chest. "I don't want to be a mistake, Tom. I can't... I can't do this if it's just going to end up being another thing that's wrong."

His hands drop, and he takes a step back, the warmth between us replaced by a cold rush of uncertainty. "Clara, you're not—"

I don't let him finish. I turn away, my head spinning, and all I can think is that I'm in over my head, again, tangled up in something I'm not ready to deal with, again. I retreat to my room, closing the door behind me with a soft click, my back pressed against it as I try to catch my breath.

Whatever this is, it's more than I bargained for, and I don't know if I'm strong enough to see it through. But the lingering taste of him, the feel of his lips on mine—it's enough to make me wish I was.

10

TOM

THE SNOW CRUNCHES under my boots as I make my way towards the main area of the hotel, the white mountain looming above me, a sharp contrast against the gray sky. It's the kind of day that feels heavy with the promise of more snow, the kind of way that I would have welcomed back in the day, eager to get out and spend all my time outside focusing on my job and whatever came with it.

My chest is tight, my mind replaying the kiss over and over—the feel of her lips against mine, the way she melted into me, like she'd been waiting for this just as much as I had.

But then she pulled away. And I let her.

I run a hand through my hair, frustration gnawing

at the edges of my thoughts. What the hell was I thinking? Kissing her like that, crossing a line I'd promised myself I wouldn't. If Ellie were here, none of this would have happened, so why am I suddenly searching for her everywhere? Like she's the puzzle piece that has been missing all along? And I'm not supposed to want this, want her, especially when I've got my life in shambles and she's just trying to figure out hers.

But that's exactly what got me into this mess, letting work take over my life, letting distance grow between me and the people I care about, until all I had left was a hollowed-out version of what I thought my life should be.

And now here I am again, on the edge of something I can't name, something that feels good in a way I haven't let myself feel in a long time.

I head down the trail toward the ski rental shop in the lower level of the hotel, trying to clear my head. The lodge is bustling with guests—families putting on snow gear, kids dragging their parents toward the slopes, and couples laughing over shared cups of hot chocolate. It's the kind of scene that should feel warm because it's exactly why I came here in the first place, but today it only makes the emptiness stand out more. I should be here with Ellie, showing her how to ski, watching her face light up at her first run down the bunny hill. Instead, she's a thousand miles away, and

I'm stuck in this villa, tangled up in feelings I shouldn't be having.

I walk aimlessly for a while, the cold air sharp against my cheeks, until I find myself back in the room. I hesitate at the door, half hoping Clara will still be in her room, that I can avoid whatever conversation we're bound to have.

But when I step inside, she's there, sitting at the kitchen table with her laptop open, a pair of reading glasses perched on her nose. She looks up when I enter and her cheeks flush slightly, but her expression remains guarded, and I can see the wall she's put up, the one I'm starting to recognize all too well.

"Hey," I say, my voice rough and gravelly. I drop my jacket on the back of a chair, my movements stiff, awkward, like I don't know how to fit in this space anymore.

"Hey," she replies, and the room is filled with a heavy, deafening silence. She closes her laptop and fiddles with the edge of her sweater, her fingers twisting the fabric like she's trying to keep herself from unraveling. "I didn't mean to just...leave like that earlier."

"It's fine," I say quickly, though we both know it's not. "I shouldn't have—"

"Let's not," she cuts in, her voice tight, and I can see the flicker in her eyes—fear, maybe, or regret, or something she's not ready to name. "We don't have to…"

"Oh, but we do," I say, because I can't just let it go. Not when she's right here, looking at me like she's waiting for something, like she's just as lost as I am. "Clara, we can't keep pretending this isn't happening." The words come out more urgent than I mean them to. "Whatever this is, whatever we're doing, we need to figure it out."

She looks at me, her eyes searching mine, and for a moment, I think she might agree. But then she shakes her head, her expression crumbling into something pained. "I don't want to be that girl, Tom. The one who gets caught up in something she knows isn't hers to have."

I flinch, her words hitting harder than I expect. "You're not—"

"Am I?" she interrupts, her voice breaking, and suddenly all that bravado is gone, replaced by a raw vulnerability that guts me. "Because I don't even know who you are, really. I don't know who you're talking to on the phone or what you're trying to get away from. And you don't know me either, not really."

She's right. I don't know anything about her, but I might just know enough. I know the way she laughs when she's nervous. The way she lights up when she talks about something she loves. The way she looks at me like she's afraid of what she might find. And I know what it feels to want her, even when I shouldn't.

"Go to dinner with me," I blurt, the last bit of desperation finally bubbling up my chest. "Tonight."

"No," she replies, her eyes firmly on me. "I already told you I'm not going to be that girl."

"I didn't plan for this," I admit, my voice dropping, and it's the closest I've come to being honest about how much she's gotten under my skin. "I didn't plan for you."

Clara stands, crossing her arms over her chest like she's trying to hold herself together. "I didn't plan for you either," she says quietly, and there's a flicker of something in her eyes that makes my chest ache. "And now I don't know what to do."

I take a step towards her, closing the gap between us. She doesn't move, doesn't back away this time. We're close, too close, and I can feel the pull again, the way everything else seems to fade when she's near.

"Give me a shot," I whisper, my hand reaching up to cup her cheek, my thumb brushing against her skin. "Just…"

She leans into my touch, her eyes fluttering closed, and for a moment, it's like everything else falls away. The uncertainty, the doubts, all of it fades into the background, leaving just us, tangled up in something that is totally undefined.

"I can't," she whispers against my hand, and her eyes flutter as the words spill out.

"Clara," I say with a sigh. "Just dinner. I mean, we don't know anyone else in this town. Might as well enjoy a meal together."

She tilts her head and looks at me in the eyes, her eyes blinking rapidly, but the silence around us stretches. It's almost as if I could hear her thoughts, her brain going through every scenario and an imaginary list of pros and cons immediately. "It's Valentine's Day."

"So?"

"I don't know." She's hesitating, and I understand why. This is temporary. We're here for a limited amount of time and we definitely didn't plan for this. I wanted to come up with a plan for a career switch—maybe a nonprofit that works to rehabilitate retired horses to use them for therapy or to give them a second chance at a fulfilling life after they're done with their athletic stints.

"It's just dinner," I say as I take a step back, tucking my hands into my pockets. "And I'll tell you all about my horses."

"Okay," she says, and it's just one word, but it's enough.

For now.

11

CLARA

I STARE at my reflection in the mirror, trying to convince myself that I haven't completely lost my mind. The soft glow of the lamp casts a warm light on my face, and I swipe on another coat of mascara, hoping it will mask the uncertainty lingering in my eyes.

I shouldn't be doing this. Going to dinner with Tom on Valentine's Day feels reckless, impulsive like stepping off a ledge without looking at what's below. When he asked, something in his voice pulled at me, and after thinking it through, I said yes. But resolved that nothing would come out of it, just a nice dinner with the excuse that it's Valentine's Day and no one wants to be alone on such a disgustingly romantic day.

Now, with my hair curled loosely around my shoulders and a simple red dress hugging my curves, I feel exposed in a way I didn't expect.

The dress is new, one I bought on a whim before this trip, thinking maybe I'd wear it to a fancy dinner or just to feel like myself again. I smooth my hands over the fabric, trying to calm the flutter of nerves in my stomach. But it's not nerves; it's something more complicated, something I haven't—won't—let myself name.

I look at myself one last time, taking a deep breath. "Okay," I whisper to my reflection. "You can do this. Just a little adventure."

But as I make my way downstairs, I hear Tom's voice, low and soft, carrying from the living room. I slow my steps, the nervous excitement in my chest twisting into something colder. He's on the phone, and I don't need to hear the words to know who he's talking to. The tone is unmistakable—gentle, warm, a side of him that he doesn't show often.

"Yes, honey," Tom says, his voice tinged with a sweetness that makes my chest tighten. "I know, princess. I miss you, too."

I stop mid-step, gripping the railing so hard my knuckles turn white. There it is again—that affectionate lilt in his voice, the kind that sends my mind spiraling. I thought I could ignore it, pretend it didn't bother me, but hearing it now, right before heading out to dinner together, feels like a punch to the gut.

"It's definitely not the same without you here," Tom continues, oblivious to the way my heart is clenching.

I can't take it anymore. I step down the last few stairs, my heels clicking loudly against the wood, and Tom glances up, startled. His phone is still pressed to his ear, but his eyes widen when he sees me. For a second, he looks guilty, like he's been caught doing something he shouldn't.

"Yeah, I'll call you tomorrow," he says quickly into the phone, his gaze never leaving mine. "Love you."

He ends the call, and the silence that follows is thick and suffocating. I cross my arms over my chest, trying to hold myself together as anger and confusion swirl inside me.

"You look—"

"Who were you talking to?"

Tom hesitates, his brows furrowing as if he's trying to gauge how much to say. "Just—just checking in."

"With who?" I press, my voice sharper than I intend. "Your girlfriend? Your wife?"

Tom's eyes widen, and he opens his mouth, but no words come out. He's caught off guard, and it just makes my frustration bubble over. I've been second-guessing everything—this trip, my choices, this stupid attraction to him—and now, it feels like all the pieces are finally coming together in the worst possible way.

"Clara, it's not—"

"Not what?" I snap, stepping closer. "Not what it looks like? Because it looks a lot like you've been sneaking around, calling someone honey, acting like you're not...I don't know...committed?"

He runs a hand through his hair, his expression twisting into something pained. "It's not like that."

"Then what is it?" I demand, my voice cracking under the weight of everything I've been holding back. "Because I don't want to be this person again—the one who gets caught up in something she doesn't understand. I don't want to be that girl, Tom. And I told you, repeatedly. But stupid little old Clara, none the wiser. You know? Not even two months ago, my boyfriend of six years got married to someone he'd met in college. They saw each other by chance and the very next day he broke up with me. Then, the man—boy, really—I dated after him broke up with me and married the girl he started dating after me, all in the span of eight months. And this past November, I found out that the man—another boy—I'd been dating for almost a year had been engaged the whole time. So please, tell me exactly what it's like."

He takes a deep breath, his gaze fixed on the floor as if searching for the right words. When he finally speaks, his voice is quieter, tinged with a vulnerability I haven't heard before. "I was talking to my daughter."

The room falls silent, and I blink, taken aback. Of all the things I was expecting him to say, this wasn't one of them. I open my mouth, but nothing comes out. My thoughts are a tangled mess, trying to catch up with the reality of what he's just revealed.

"Your daughter?" I echo, my voice small, almost disbelieving.

"Yeah," Tom says, his shoulders slumping, like he's been carrying this weight for far too long. "Ellie, Elizabeth. She's nine. She was supposed to be here with me, but she got snowed in in New York with her mom. We had this whole trip planned and now..." He trails off, his eyes clouded with guilt and regret.

I stand there, stunned. Suddenly, everything I've been feeling—jealousy, confusion, anger—feels misplaced, like I've been fighting a battle that didn't even exist. I swallow hard, trying to process it all. "Why didn't you just tell me?"

Tom shrugs, his expression pained. "I don't know. I guess I just... I didn't want to bring it up. This trip was supposed to be for her, for us. I've been divorced for five years, and it's been... It's been hard, you know? Balancing everything. And I didn't want you to think —" He stops, taking a shaky breath. "I didn't want you to think I was some mess dragging my kid into all this."

I soften at his words, the raw honesty in them. I can see now that he's been trying to shield something precious, and the weight of it all is written in the lines of his face. "I'm sorry," I say quietly, guilt washing over me. "I just... I thought—"

"You thought I was hiding something," he finished for me, nodding slowly. "And I was. Just not what you thought."

We stand there, a fragile silence stretching between us. I don't know what to say, how to bridge the gap that's grown between us over something that never should have been a secret in the first place. I look at Tom, at the weariness in his eyes, and I realize he's not the polished, put-together guy I first assumed.

"Almost four years ago, my then-boyfriend and I were visiting his hometown to celebrate his grandmother's eightieth birthday. We'd been together for years, living together for two of them at that point."

Tom nods, taking a step closer to me, but I stop him with my hand, because I want to get this out. I've only spoken to a handful of people about this—no one really knows the exact details of that breakup, but something in the way he's looking at me makes me compelled to tell him.

"One day, literally out of the blue, he breaks up with me. Like, I did not see it coming at all. As a matter of fact, I thought we were going to get married. One minute I'm sitting in his parents' house having coffee, the next, I'm on a bus headed back to the city to move out of our place. And I had to move back to my parents' house, which is not that big of a deal, but it did a number on my confidence. Like, how delusional was I that I thought I was going to marry that guy and then the next day it was over?"

I smile, but my eyes fill with tears. I'm definitely over that breakup, but it did so much to my confidence that I'm not yet recovered.

"Come to find out, his college crush showed up to his hometown by a complete act of coincidence and, I don't know, he saw a chance? Didn't want to get confused, so he got rid of me, just like that." I snap my fingers. "They got married, and she moved to his tiny small town, something we had never even discussed and I would have done in a heartbeat."

"Shit," he mutters as he reaches for my hand. "I'm sorry."

"And every person I've dated since, for the past three years or so once I've decided to get back out there, has found *the one* immediately after they broke up with me. Some of them while we were together. So, like...get where I'm coming from? I never know if it's real or not. If they've been seeing someone behind my back or they really aren't that much into me, or never really loved me..."

"Oh, Jesus," he adds, and pulls me towards him, our bodies colliding. "I'm so sorry."

I nod, feeling the weight of his words settle in my chest.

"It's been a difficult few years," I say with a sad smile. "And it's been one after the other, and it's hit me like a bag of bricks. So then, as you can imagine, I come here to this paradise on earth to *find myself*," I say as I roll my eyes, "and end up finding something—someone—else. And I'm so confused..."

"Same." He chuckles, lifting his hand and tucking a strand of my hair behind my ear.

"You love her a lot," I say softly, my voice filled with an understanding I didn't have before.

"More than anything," Tom replies, his voice rough. "She's my whole world. But my job...it takes me everywhere. And I don't want to be away from her, but I have to be, and it's just... It's a mess."

"I get it," I say, and I mean it.

Tom looks at me, his eyes searching mine, and for the first time, there's no pretense, no walls. Just him, laid bare, struggling to keep it all together. "I didn't mean to drag you like this," he admits, his voice barely above a whisper. "I didn't plan for any of this."

"Neither did I," I say, and it's the truth. I didn't plan for any of this—this trip, this villa, this man who's become so much more than a stranger sharing my space. I take a step closer, closing the already small gap between us. "But I'm glad we're here."

Tom's eyes soften and he cups my cheek. It's a simple touch, but it feels like a promise, like maybe we can figure this out, even if my trip ends in six days. "So am I," he says, his thumb brushing gently under my eye. "So am I."

12

CLARA

THE TOWN IS a vision of romance—heart-shaped garlands draped from every awning, twinkling lights illuminating the snow-dusted pathways, and couples bundled up, strolling hand in hand through the festive displays. It's all so beautiful, and it should feel ridiculous, but tonight, with Tom by my side, it feels different. Almost perfect.

We walk through the town's plaza, his hand resting gently on my lower back, guiding me toward the fancy restaurant nestled between the coffee shop and the bakery. It's a small gesture, but it sends warmth spreading through me, easing the lingering tension from our earlier conversation.

The hostess greets us with a bright smile and leads

us to a table near the window, overlooking the slopes. The view is breathtaking, the mountains bathed in the soft glow of moonlight, and for a moment, I forget about everything that's been weighing on me.

"This place is something else," I say, slipping out of my coat and settling into the pink velvet bench. The room is softly lit, the table adorned with candles and rose petals, every detail meticulously planned to set the mood. "It's like they went through a Valentine's Day catalog and bought everything they could find."

Tom chuckles, his eyes crinkling at the corners in a way that's becoming far too familiar. "Yeah, it's like Cupid exploded in here. But I guess they know their audience."

I laugh, but it's not just the decorations that are making my heart feel lighter. It's him. It's the way he's looking at me, the easy conversation that's flowed between us since we left the villa, and the quiet understanding we've started to build. It's new and unexpected, but it feels good—like slipping into a warm bath after being out in the cold for too long.

A waiter appears, dropping off menus and lighting the small candle between us. Tom's eyes flick to mine, and there's a spark there that makes my pulse quicken. "So," he says, picking up the menu, "what's your poison? And please, for the love of god, don't say jam on toast."

I snort, glancing at the options. "You're never going to let that go, are you?"

"Not a chance." He grins, and it's infectious, making me feel lighter than I have in weeks. "I'm still shocked. Honestly, I'm not sure if I should call the authorities or try to convert you."

"Well," I say, leaning back in my chair, "if this dinner is just an elaborate scheme to make me eat more eggs, I'm going to be seriously disappointed."

Tom's laugh is low and genuine, and he shakes his head, setting his menu down. "I promise, it's not. But I am going to order the French onion soup, because it's the best thing on the menu, they say, and I refuse to let you leave this place without trying it."

"Fine," I say with a dramatic sigh. "Twist my arm. I'm always up for trying new things." I'm not just talking about the soup, and I think he knows it.

We order our food, and as the waiter walks away, Tom leans in, resting his elbows on the table. "So, Clara Ledesma," he says, his voice dropping to a teasing whisper. "Tell me something about you that I don't know. Something good."

I hesitate, caught off guard by the directness of his question. It's easy to forget that we've only just scratched the surface of each other's lives, that there's so much left to uncover. "I'm a flight attendant," I say, but it comes out more like a confession. "Been doing it for years. It's kind of a family thing—my mom was one, my sister is one, too, and I guess it just felt natural. Plus, I like being in the sky, you know? Being up there, above every-thing." I make a face. "And all the traveling is nice, too."

Tom watches me, his expression thoughtful. "That sounds amazing. Must be nice to just…leave every-thing on the ground."

I nod, stirring my water with my straw. "Yeah. It's freeing. But it's also exhausting. Always being away, always feeling like you're in transit, like you never really land anywhere."

He smiles softly, a hint of understanding in his eyes. "I get that. My job's the same way. I'm always on the go, always somewhere new. It's great, but it's also…lonely sometimes."

I lean forward, intrigued. "What do you do, exactly? I've been dying to ask but didn't want to seem nosy. Especially because we started off on the wrong foot and… you know."

Tom rubs the back of his neck, a sheepish smile crossing his face. "I work with horses. I used to play polo professionally, up until a few years ago, and now I'm more on the horse-breeding side?" His answer comes out as a question, as if he's trying to explain to himself what he's doing. "There's so much that goes into play when we are talking about polo horses, it's fascinating. But it's also a lot of travel, a lot of moving pieces. A lot of competition and very, very high standards."

"Wow," I say, genuinely impressed. "That sounds... intense."

"It is," he admits, his gaze flicking to the window for a moment, like he's lost in thought. "It's not as rewarding as I thought it would be, unfortunately. It's just taking me away from Ellie, so I'm trying to figure out if this is what I should continue to do or not."

I nod, understanding the meaning behind his words. I can see it in his eyes, the way he talks about his work and his daughter. It's maybe turned into just a job for him now—not something that drives him, that makes all the sacrifices worth it. And I get it. I've felt that, too, they way flying used to make me feel invincible, like I was chasing something just out of reach, but at what expense?

"I've been thinking more and more about maybe making a switch. I spoke with my business partner right before this trip and with the whole solo fiasco, I... I was supposed to use this time to come up with a plan for slowly selling my part to him and maybe starting something else. Use my connections in the polo world to maybe set up some sort of stables or something to rehab retired horses and use them for therapy or for riding lessons, or even for polo but at a lower, more amateur level."

I gasp, and he smiles, the movement reaching his eyes. "That sounds exciting."

"Yes, and I'm warming up to the idea more and more." He's so handsome, even in this ultra pink restaurant, the ceiling covered in faux pink flowers and heart-shaped garlands. "Ellie would love it, too."

We fall into an easy rhythm, sharing stories about our travels, laughing over the absurdities of airports and missed connections, and swapping tales of the most ridiculous passengers and clients we've dealt with. It's effortless, and I find myself leaning closer, hanging on his every word. There's something so magnetic about the way he speaks, this quiet confidence that makes me want to keep listening, to keep learning.

The waiter brings our food, and the smell of the French onion soup wafts up, rich and comforting. Tom watches as I take my first spoonful, his eyes lighting up when I let out a small, appreciative hum.

"Okay," I say, pointing my spoon at him. "You were right. This is amazing."

Tom raises his glass, a playful grin on his lips. "To good soup and unexpected company."

I clink my glass against his, smiling as I take a sip of my wine. It's so easy to be around him, to let my guard down in a way that feels dangerous and thrilling all at once. I've never had this kind of connection with someone so quickly, this immediate comfort that makes everything else fade into the background.

As we eat, the conversation dips into deeper waters, and before I know it, I'm telling him things I haven't told anyone in years—about the endless string of failed relationships, the constant feeling of not being enough, and the restless urge to keep moving, keep searching for whatever it is that's missing.

Tom listens, his attention never wavering, and when he speaks, it's with a kind of honesty that cuts right through me. "I get that," he says, his voice soft. "I've spent a lot of years thinking if I just kept moving, kept working, I wouldn't have to deal with...all the stuff I didn't want to face. But it catches up to you, you know?"

I nod, feeling the weight of his words settle in my chest. "Yeah. It does."

There is a lull in the conversation, the kind that should feel awkward but doesn't. I look at Tom, really look at him, and I realize that I've never felt this kind of easy with anyone. Not even with Santiago, who was such a wonderful man, and our relationship was good —until it wasn't.

It scares me how much I want to reach across the table and touch him, to close the distance between us.

"Clara," Tom says, his voice drawing me back. "I'm glad we're doing this. I know it's complicated, but I'm glad."

"Me, too," I admit, my heart pounding in my chest. And I mean it. Being here, in this cozy little restaurant, surrounded by too many Valentine's Day decorations, feels like exactly where I'm supposed to be.

But then, as if the universe is reminding me not to get too comfortable, the waiter comes to our table, a giant grin on his face and a plate with chocolate cake in his hand. What is it with people in this town and their secretive, conspiratorial smiles? Tom's eyes widen, and we both burst out laughing, the tension between us breaking like a dam.

"No," he says quickly to the waiter, who is about to place the dessert in front of me. His expression is so mischievous, it has to mean that he's hiding a secret. "I don't think that's for us."

"Oh my god," I say between fits of giggles, wiping a tear from my eye. "This is so over the top. I can't believe it happened again."

Tom shakes his head, still laughing. "I swear I didn't plan this. But if you start crying, I'm going to have to get on one knee."

"Oh, please don't," I gasp, clutching my sides. "I can't handle a grand gesture today."

Tom extends his hand in my direction, placing it on the table, and I follow. His hand wraps around mine and we sit there, looking at each other like two fools in love. "Would this be an acceptable place to propose, then?"

I look around for the first time at the other tables. Everyone is sitting down, laughing, smiling, enjoying their food, in their own little universes. Just like we are.

"So?" He smiles widely, his brown eyes shining even in the dim light. "What do you say?"

"If you had proposed today, I would have said no."

"Good to know. I'll keep that in mind." He smiles.

We talk and laugh until our cheeks hurt, and as the evening flies by, it feels like the world has shrunk to just the two of us. The night could end right here, in this perfect little bubble, and it would be enough. But I can't help the sinking feeling that whatever this is, whatever we're building, has an expiration date.

Six days. That's all we have. And as much as I want to forget that, to lose myself in the moment, I know it's there, hovering just out of sight.

For now, though, I let it go. I focus on Tom, on the way his eyes light up when he laughs, and I let myself believe, just for tonight, that this could be more than just a beautiful, fleeting mistake.

13

CLARA

THE NIGHT AIR is crisp and biting as we step out of the restaurant, a shiver running down my spine despite the warmth still lingering from our dinner. Tom's hand finds the small of my back again, steadying me as we navigate the icy path back toward the villa. The snow crunches beneath our feet, and the world around us feels quiet, like it's holding its breath.

We walk in a comfortable silence, the kind that doesn't need filling, and every time I glance over at him, he's looking at me with this soft, almost disbelieving smile that sends my heart racing. The town glows under the soft, muted lights of streetlamps, and everything feels magical, like we're the only two people in the world.

"Did you have fun?" Tom asks, breaking the silence as we approach the steps to the villa. He's got that lopsided grin again, the one that makes me feel like he's genuinely happy, like this isn't just another night out.

"I did," I admit, feeling the warmth of his hand through my thick coat. And it's the truth. "More than I thought I would."

He raises an eyebrow, mock offended. "Hey, I can be fun, you know."

I laugh, rolling my eyes. "I never said you couldn't."

We reach the door, and for a second, I hesitate. The night could end here, neatly tied up with a polite goodnight and a friendly wave. It would be the sensible thing to do—the smart thing. But there's something about the way Tom looks at me, the unspoken promise in his eyes, that makes me linger.

He unlocks the door, and we step inside, the villa's warmth enveloping us immediately. I kick off my heels, feeling the familiar tug of uncertainty pulling at my mind. This is usually the part where I second-guess myself, where I make an excuse to leave before things get messy. But tonight, I don't want to leave. I don't want to over-think. I just want to be here, in this moment, with him.

Tom slips off his coat and hangs it on the rack by the door, his movements slow and deliberate, like he's stalling for time. He turns to me, his gaze lingering a little too long, and I can feel the tension between us, electric and charged.

"Do you want a drink or something?" he asks, his voice quieter than before, like he's not sure if he should even be offering. "Or...I don't know."

"I'm good," I say softly, taking a step closer to him. There's barely half a meter of space between us now, and I can feel the heat radiating off his body, pulling me like a magnet.

We're standing in the middle of the living room, the soft glow of the fireplace casting shadows across his face. I can see every line, every contour, and there's a tenderness there that makes my heart ache. This man, who I barely knew less than a week ago, feels like something familiar and foreign all at once.

"Tom," I whisper, but I don't know what I'm about to say. All I know is that I'm caught between wanting to hold on and wanting to let go, and he's the only thing anchoring me.

He reaches out, his hand brushing against my cheek, and the contact sends a shiver through me. "Clara," he says, his voice low, almost reverent. "I..."

Whatever he's about to say is lost as I close the gap between us, pressing my lips to his in a kiss that feels like it's been building for days. It's slow at first, tentative, both of us testing the waters, but then his arms wrap around me, pulling me closer, and everything else fades away.

I can feel the steady thump of his heartbeat against my chest, and it's grounding, reassuring in a way I didn't expect. His hands move to my waist, sliding up my back, and I lose myself in the taste of him, the way he sighs into the kiss, like he's been waiting for this just as long as I have.

We stumble back, knocking into the coffee table, and I let out a breathless laugh, the sound breaking the intensity of the moment. Tom grins against my lips, and there's something playful in his eyes, something that makes me want to keep going, to see where this will take us.

"Sorry," he murmurs, but there's no real apology in his voice. He's not sorry at all, and neither am I.

"Don't be," I whisper back, my fingers threading through his hair. "Don't you dare be."

We move together, inching our way toward the massive couch, our kisses growing more urgent, more desperate. Tom's hands are everywhere—cupping my face, skimming down my sides, holding me like he's afraid I might slip away. I feel alive, every nerve ending tingling with the thrill of being this close to him, of finally giving in to what's been simmering between us.

He sits down on the couch, pulling me onto his lap, and I straddle him, my dress hitching up as I press closer. His breath is warm against my neck, and I arch into him, my fingers digging into his shoulders as he trails kisses along my collarbone.

"Clara," he murmurs, his voice thick with want. "Tell me if this is too much."

I shake my head, my own breath ragged. "It's not. I want this, I want you."

The admission feels big, too big, but it's the truth. I want him, every messy, complicated part of him. And for tonight, and maybe the rest of this trip, that's enough.

We move together, our bodies finding a rhythm that feels natural, like we've done this a thousand times before. His hands are firm on my hips, guiding me, and I can feel the tension building between us, a tight coil ready to snap.

I kiss him again, deeper this time, pouring every ounce of need into it, and he responds with a fervor that takes my breath away. It's all heat and urgency, a clash of lips and tangled limbs, and I can't get enough.

Tom's fingers slide under the hem of my dress, skimming the skin of my thighs, and I shiver at the contact, leaning into his touch. It's like nothing I've ever felt before—this mix of tenderness and desire, of wanting and being wanted.

"You're so wet," he whispers, his voice low and gravelly in my ear, and my cheeks flush. I should be embarrassed, but instead, I feel empowered. Brazen, even. This is what it's like to be with someone who truly sees you, I realize. "Fuck."

He slides a finger inside me, and I moan, arching my back and pressing myself against him. Tom's touch is reverent, slow, like he's exploring every inch of me, memorizing the way I feel, the way I taste. I cling to him, my nails digging into his back as the sensations building within me grow stronger, more insistent.

"Tom," I gasp out, my voice barely above a whimper, and he groans in response, his pace quickening. Heat pools between my thighs, and I know I'm close, so close.

Tom's kisses trail down my neck, over my collarbone, and over my breasts as his other hand slides up my waist, tracing a path up my chest, sending shivers down my spine. His touch is electric, making me feel alive in a way I never have before. My body responds to his touch unpredictably, writhing under him as he circles his hips, thrusting his fingers deeper and harder. I grip his shoulders tightly, my nails digging into his skin as I try to hold on to this feeling; it's as if I'm flying above the surface, no landing in sight.

My breath hitches when I feel a second finger glide effortlessly into my core, stretching me further than I thought possible. He cups one of my breasts over my dress, his thumb rubbing gently over my nipple, sending sparks of pleasure throughout my body.

"You like that?" Tom rasps, his breathing heavy in my ear.

I cry out, arching my back, begging for more. He answers by thrusting his fingers in and out of me in a rhythmic motion, drawing out my pleasure until it's all-consuming.

My breath comes in ragged gasps as I feel myself spiraling towards the edge. And then, with one final hard push, I'm overcome. I scream Tom's name as my body shudders with the force of my orgasm, my walls gripping his fingers tightly as if they're all that's keeping me grounded.

Panting heavily, I collapse against him, feeling boneless and unsure of what just happened. But he isn't done yet. He lifts me up in his arms, wrapping my legs around his waist and flying up the stairs until we're in the bedroom, kicking the door closed behind us. He lays me down gently on the bed, and before I can gather my thoughts, he's kissing me again, his lips demanding and possessive.

And they are everywhere—my neck, my shoulders, the curve of my hip—and I arch into him, my hands roaming over the expanse of his toned back, feeling the flex of muscle under my touch. I want to memorize every inch of him, every sigh and shudder, every whispered "Clara" that slips from his lips.

14

TOM

SHE RETURNS MY KISS, matching my intensity, and I strip off my clothes, revealing my body. Her eyes widen and her gaze moves, from my stomach to my eyes and then back down to my erection, hard and angry and ready for her.

She bites her lower lip, and I can't help but groan. I slide my hand up her thigh, and she shivers again. Her skin is soft, silky.

"Fuck, you're gorgeous," I breathe, my voice husky with desire. I can't take my eyes off her splayed form, her beauty, her curves. I need to explore every inch of her, to memorize her, etch her into my flesh.

With infinite patience, I trail my fingertips up her thigh, over her hip, and then ever so gently, I brush the side of her breasts as I remove her red dress. She arches her back, pressing into my touch.

"Tom," she moans, her voice raw with need.

"Clara," I whisper into her skin, and then I'm on her, kissing her nipple, sucking, teasing with my tongue. Her taste is intoxicating. I trail my kisses down her stomach, leaving a path of goosebumps in my wake.

I can feel her trembling beneath me, and it stirs a deeper anticipation within me.

I hook my fingers into her underwear and slide them down her legs. My cock twitches in response. I look up at her, arching my eyebrows.

"Do you have a condom?" she asks, her voice shaky, her pupils dilated. Her hands are fisting the comforter and the longer I stare, the more she squirms under me.

"Yeah," I rasp, reaching for my wallet. I tear open the packet, sheathing myself. I meet her eyes, and I see the want, the need, but also the trust. Trust in me, in us. I hope I don't disappoint her.

Slowly, I guide myself inside her, and as our hips touch, I stop. I look at her, and she nods, her breathing erratic. I push in a little more, and her walls clench around me. She's so tight, so hot, and I groan.

"Jesus, Clara," I growl, and I can feel her smile against my neck.

Inch by inch, I ease myself into her, savoring every

sensation. Her nails dig into my back, and I thrust in deeper, until I can't go any further. Tight and wet and perfect.

"Tom," she whimpers, her hips bucking against mine.

"You feel so good, sweetheart," I say, and I start to move, slowly at first and then a little bit faster. Her moans spur me on, and soon, we're moving together in a rhythm that feels natural, like we've done this before.

"Right there," she whispers in my ear, and she moans as I thrust into her, arching her back every time I'm fully inside her. "Yes, yes," she pants, her head thrown back. She's so beautiful with her hair splayed around her and her cheeks flushed. There's a light sheen of sweat on her forehead that I'm tempted to lick.

"God, you feel so good, so tight," I groan, my body tense with the effort it takes not to lose control, and the way she's moving beneath me, I don't know how much longer I can last.

"Don't stop, don't stop," she chants, tightening around me. "I'm so close."

That's all I need to hear. I start to move faster, harder, and she's right there with me, her hips matching me. She wraps her long legs around my hips and pushes my body against her with her feet, holding on tight so that I can barely move.

"Oh, fuck, Clara, I'm going to—"

That's all I manage to say before I lose myself, my orgasm tearing through me, my entire body on fire. I collapse on top of her, my heart pounding in my ears, and she's panting beneath me, her face buried in my shoulder, muffling the soft gasp that escapes her lips.

I shift, rolling onto my side, and pull her into my chest. She nestles against me, as I feel the steady rise and fall of her breathing, and I close my eyes, letting the warmth of her body lull me into a contented daze.

The room is dark, save for the soft moonlight filtering through the curtains. The heat of the moment still lingers in the air, wrapping around us like a heavy blanket. I run my fingers gently through Clara's hair, trying to steady my own breathing, still riding the high of everything that just happened.

I don't know how long we've been lying here, tangled in sheets and each other, but it feels like no time at all and forever at the same time. I glance down at Clara; her eyes are closed, her face serene, and for a moment, I wonder if she's fallen asleep. But then she shifts, her hand moving to trace lazy patterns on my chest, and I feel her smile against my skin.

"That was..." she begins, her voice trailing off as she searches for the right words.

I chuckle, my chest rumbling beneath her. "Yeah. It was."

She lifts her head, popping herself up on one

elbow to look at me. Her hair is a wild mess, her cheeks flushed, and she looks impossibly beautiful. I reach out, tucking a strand of hair behind her ear. "You look so smug right now," she says, narrowing her eyes at me, but there's no real bite behind it.

"Can you blame me?" I tease, grinning like a damn fool. "I think I've earned it."

She laughs, a soft sound that makes my chest tighten. It's light, airy, like a burst of bubbles that fills the room. "Okay, maybe just a little," she admits, biting her lip in that way that drives me absolutely crazy. She shifts, pulling the sheet up over her chest, suddenly shy despite everything.

I roll onto my side, propping my head up with my hand, so I can look at her properly. "You're incredible, you know that?"

She rolls her eyes, but there's a blush creeping up her neck. "I'm pretty sure that's just the post-sex glow talking."

"Maybe," I concede, but my smile softens. "But I mean it. You're…"

She doesn't say anything at first, just watches me with those blue eyes that seem to see right through me. It's unnerving and comforting all at once, the way she looks at me like I'm more than just this mess of a man who's been trying to hold his life together with duct tape and good intentions.

"What are we doing, Tom?" she finally asks, her

voice small but laced with curiosity. "This wasn't supposed to happen."

I let out a breath, reaching for her hand and lacing our fingers together. "I don't know," I admit honestly. "But whatever this is, it feels...right. Doesn't it?"

She nods, but there's a flicker of uncertainty in her eyes. "Yeah, it does. But it's also...complicated. And temporary."

Her words hang between us, heavy with the truth I've been trying to ignore since the moment I met her. This isn't forever, not even close. We're here in this bubble. But at some point, it's going to burst, and we'll have to go back to our separate lives, in opposite corners of the world. The thought sends a pang of something I don't want to acknowledge through my chest.

"I've never been good at this stuff," I admit, my voice barely above a whisper. "Relationships, I mean. Erin, my ex-wife, used to say I was married to my job first and her second, and she wasn't wrong. When I was playing polo, I really didn't understand what she was talking about. But since I've transitioned to this behind-the-scenes role... I've been trying to figure out how to do it differently, but it's hard when your life is on the road, and you're always chasing something just out of reach."

Clara watches me, her gaze softening, and I see a flicker of understanding there. "I get that," she says, her voice gentle. "I've realized you can't outrun yourself forever."

I nod, squeezing her hand. "Yeah. That's exactly it."

We fall into a comfortable silence, and for the first time in a long time, I feel like I'm not alone in this. Like maybe there's someone who understands the mess of it all, the struggle of trying to figure out who you are when you're constantly on the move, no time or headspace to stop and think.

"You ever think about just...stopping? I mean, not slowly thinking of tapering off but rather just..." Clara asks, her voice barely above a whisper. "Like, giving it all up and starting over somewhere new? Completely new, where no one knows you."

I turn my head to look at her, and she's staring up at the ceiling like she's lost in some far-off thought. "Every day," I confess, and it feels like a weight lifting off my chest to say it out loud. "And I've got Ellie to think about. I don't want her to grow up thinking her dad's always chasing something more important than her. I want to be there for her, even if I don't always know how to do that. And I think, in part, this horse stables idea is in response to that feeling. Obviously, it's not perfect yet, but it could be a good start."

Clara's eyes meet mine, and she nods slowly, a soft smile tugging at her lips. "She's lucky to have you."

I shrug, feeling a familiar pang of guilt. "I don't

know about that. Half the time, I feel like I'm just screwing it all up."

"You're not," Clara says firmly, her fingers squeezing mine. "You're doing the best you can, and that's all anyone can ask for."

I swallow hard, her words hitting me in a way I wasn't expecting. There's a vulnerability in her voice, a quiet kind of strength that makes me realize just how much I needed to hear that. I pull her closer, pressing a kiss to her forehead, and she melts into me, her warmth seeping into my bones.

"You ever wonder why we met?" I ask, my voice muffled against her hair. "Like, what the hell kind of twist of fate brought us here?"

Clara laughs softly, her breath tickling my chest. "Oh, I've stopped trying to figure that out. I've decided the universe is just messing with me at this point."

"Probably," I agree, my fingers tracing lazy circles on her back. "But I'm glad it did. Mess with you, I mean."

She tilts her head up to look at me, her eyes searching mine. "Yeah," she says, her voice barely audible. "Me, too."

15

CLARA

THE MORNING LIGHT seeps through the cracks in the curtains, painting soft lines across the bed and illuminating the room in a hazy, golden glow. I blink against the brightness, my mind still foggy with the remnants of sleep and the warm weight of Tom's arm draped over my waist. His breath is even, soft against the back of my neck, and for a moment, I let myself just lie there, sinking into the comfort of his presence.

This isn't how I imagined waking up this morning. In fact, I didn't imagine waking up next to him at all. But here we are, tangled up in each other, the sheets twisted around our legs like they're trying to keep us from moving, from breaking whatever spell this is.

I shift slightly, trying not to wake him, but his arm

tightens around me, pulling me closer, and I can feel the steady beat of his heart against my back. I close my eyes, biting back a smile. It feels good—too good—and that's the part that scares me. I've been here before, in this space between hope and reality, and I've been burned more times than I can count.

But Tom isn't like the others. He's different. I knew that from the first moment he offered me coffee in the kitchen, his asshole exterior hiding something softer, something real. And last night, when he looked at me like I was the only person in the world, I believed it. I believed him.

I turn in his arms, careful not to disturb him, and find myself face-to-face with a version of Tom I haven't seen before—soft, unguarded, still asleep with his hair a tousled mess and his stubble shadowing his jaw. He looks younger like this, all the worries and stress smoothed out, and it hits me just how vulnerable this moment is, sharing this space with me.

I reach out, my fingers tracing the curve of his cheek, and his eyes flutter open, sleepy and unfocused. For a second, he just blinks at me, like he's not quite sure if I'm real or if he's still dreaming, and then his lips curl into a slow, lazy smile.

"Hey," he says, his voice thick with sleep, and there's something so endearing about the way he says it, like it's the first word he's ever spoken.

"Hey," I whisper back, my thumb brushing over his bottom lip. "Did you sleep okay?"

He nods, stretching like a contented cat, his muscles rippling under the sheets. "Yeah. Best sleep I've had in a while."

"Same," I admit, and it's the truth. "And this coming from a flight attendant that is regularly sleep deprived and can, almost literally, fall asleep anywhere."

I look at him, my eyes moving to study his face in the early morning light. I can't remember the last time I felt this at ease, this...safe. It's a strange feeling, and I don't know what to do with it.

Tom shifts, propping himself up on one elbow to look at me, and his eyes are bright and curious. "What's going on in that head of yours?"

I laugh softly, shaking my head. "Nothing. Everything. I don't know." I bite my lip, feeling suddenly shy under his gaze. "Just...thinking."

"About?" he prompts his thumb tracing idle circles on my hip.

I hesitate, chewing on my bottom lip as I try to find the right words. "This. What happens after."

The questions hangs between us, heavy and unavoidable, and Tom's smile fades, replaced by something more serious. "I've been thinking about that, too."

I nod, swallowing hard. "This is... This is temporary, right? We go back to our lives, and this is just a nice—super nice," I say with a smile, "memory."

Tom's brow furrows, and he looks at me like he's trying to figure something out, like he's weighing his options. "It doesn't have to be."

My heart skips a beat, and I force myself to look away, my gaze fixed on the sliver of sunlight creeping across the floor. I wonder if he got up last night to close the blinds before we drifted off to sleep. "Tom, you have a life. A daughter. I'm just... I'm just a detour."

"You're not a detour," he says, his voice firm, and I can feel his eyes on me, burning with intensity. "You're not some pit stop on my way back to reality. You're—" He pauses, struggling to find the words, and when he finally speaks, his voice is quieter, more vulnerable. "Maybe you're exactly what I didn't know I needed."

I close my eyes, feeling the weight of his words settle in my chest. "That's sweet, but..."

"But?" He encourages, and there's a hint of frustration there.

"But it's not that simple. You're a great guy, Tom, but we live in different worlds. And when this ends—because it has to end—I don't want to be the girl who can't let go."

Tom reaches out, cupping my face in his hands, and I can see the determination in his eyes. "What if it doesn't have to end?"

I open my mouth to argue, to list all the reasons why this can't work, but then he kisses me, slow and deliberate, like he's trying to erase every doubt from my mind. And for a moment, it works. I melt into him, my hands tangling in his hair, and all the reasons not to do this fade into the background.

When he pulls back, his forehead resting against mine, he sighs. "Clara, I know it's complicated. I know we've got a lot to figure out. But I'm willing to try if you are."

I blink up at him, my heart pounding in my chest. "And what does trying look like?"

He smiles, a little unsure, but there's hope in his eyes. "I don't know yet. But maybe we take it one day at a time. See where this goes."

I nod, feeling something crack open inside me, something I've been trying to keep locked away for the past four years. "Okay," I reply, "one day at a time."

Tom grins, and it's like the sun breaking through the clouds. "Good. Because I'm not done with you yet."

And before I can process his words, his lips are on mine again, and all thoughts of the future, of the complications, of the real world evaporate into the background as we lose ourselves in each other. His hands roam my body, reacquainting themselves with every curve and dip, and I can feel the heat between my legs, the desire that has been simmering between us for a while now.

Tom's hands slip under my t-shirt, his fingers skimming over my skin, goosebumps erupting in their wake. I can feel my nipples hardening, eager for his touch, and I can't remember the last time I've been this turned on. His mouth trails down my jaw, his tongue skating over my collarbone, and I can't help but arch into his touch, aching for more.

"Tom," I gasp, my voice ragged with need. His response is a growl of approval as he continues moving his hands, his fingers slipping into my shorts, seeking out my clit.

"God, you're so wet already," he mumbles against my neck, and I blush, but I can't bring myself to care. All I can focus on is the feel of his talented fingers, the way they know exactly where to touch, exactly how to send me spiraling over the edge.

"Condom," I manage to gasp, my brain foggy with lust. "In my—" He silences me with a kiss, his fingers continuing their relentless pressure as he reaches for the floor on my side of the bed, grabbing his discarded pants from the floor.

"Got it," he says, and a moment later, he's back, foil packet in hand, and I can only whimper my approval as he removes my shorts and covers my body with his.

He's slow at first, easing himself inside me, his eyes never leaving mine. "You okay?" he pants, and I nod, my walls clenching around him, trying to draw him in further. "Good," he says, his voice strained, "because I can't get enough."

And then he's moving, his hips a blur as he picks up the pace, driving deep inside me, over and over again.

I can feel the pleasure building, coiling low in my belly, and I know it won't be long. "Tom," I moan, my nails digging into his shoulders, and with a final, animalistic growl, he picks up the pace even more, his hands on my hips, guiding us towards the edge.

"Me, too," he grunts, and his movements become more frantic, his hips slamming into mine with a force that threatens to send me over the edge of the bed. "Fuck, you feel so good."

"So you've said," I barely make out, giving him a cheeky smile that doesn't last long, because just then, my world explodes, stars behind my eyelids as my climax washes over me, intense and all-consuming. Tom's name is on my lips as I come undone, and a moment later, I feel him stiffen, his body tensing as he joins me.

We stay like that for a moment, panting, our bodies entwined, until Tom finally collapses on top of me, his chest heaving. He presses a quick kiss to my temple, and I let myself sink into the moment with this man, yet again.

16

TOM

THE DAYS HAVE STARTED to blur together, each one marked by moments that feel like stolen time—Clara's laughter echoing off the walls of the villa, the quiet conversations over breakfast, and the shared silences that say more than any words ever could. It's like I've been living in a snow globe these past few days, everything outside this little bubble of ours faded into a distant hum.

But the countdown has started. Five days left. Four. Three. Each one slipping through my fingers faster than I can hold on to, and the looming reality of each of our departures feels like a ticking clock, a weight pressing against my chest. I can feel it in every second that passes, in every lingering glance and every kiss that tastes like a question we're both too afraid to ask.

I'm in the kitchen, staring blankly at the coffee machine as it hisses and steams, when Clara walks in, her hair still damp from the shower we took together and her cheeks flushed from the heat. She's wearing one of my sweatshirts, and the sight of her in my clothes does something to me that I can't put into words. It's stupid, really, but it feels like some kind of claim, like she's mine, even if just for a little while longer.

"Hi," she says, smiling as she slides onto the barstool, her fingers tapping idly on the counter. "What's the plan for today?"

I hand her a mug, watching as she takes it, her fingers brushing against mine for just a second longer than necessary. It's those little touches, those fleeting moments of connection, that have started to feel like lifelines. "I was thinking we could check out that ice skating rink you mentioned," I say, trying to sound casual, even though I've been planning out every minute of our remaining time together in my head. "You said you've never skated, right?"

Clara's eyes light up, and she takes a sip of her coffee, nodding. "Yeah, never had the chance. I always wanted to, though."

"Well, today's the day," I say, a grin tugging at my lips. "We'll make it happen."

She tilts her head, studying me for a moment like she's trying to read between the lines. "You're really cramming it all in, huh?"

I shrug, trying to play it cool, even though she's nailed it. I am cramming. I'm cramming every damn second because I don't want this to end. "Just making sure you get the full winter wonderland experience," I joke, but there's an edge to my voice that I can't hide. I have no idea how it happened or when, but she's so far under my skin that it might take surgical precision to remove her.

Clara doesn't push, but there's something in her eyes—a softness, a knowing—that makes my chest tighten. She reaches across the counter, her hand resting on mine, and it's such a simple gesture, but it grounds me. "Thanks," she says, gesturing with her other hand, "for all of this."

I clear my throat, suddenly feeling like there's too much I want to say and not enough time to say it. "Yeah, of course."

We finish our coffee in silence, the kind that's become second nature to us, and I steal glances at her from across the island. I want to memorize everything —the way her nose scrunches up when she's thinking, the way she tucks her hair behind her ear when she's nervous, the sound of her voice when she says my name. It's pathetic how much I've come to depend on these little things, and I'm not ready to let them go.

The rink is empty when we arrive, no families or couples gliding across the ice. Clara's eyes widen as she takes it all in, her excitement palpable, and it makes me smile. Seeing her like this—carefree, happy—makes everything worth it. Even if this was not the original plan and it was just happenstance... it feels right.

We rent skates and lace up at one of the benches by the ice, and I can't resist teasing her as she fumbles with the laces. "Need some help, rookie?"

Clara shoots me a playful glare, her lips curling into a smirk. "I've got it, Mr. Athlete. Just...give me a minute."

I chuckle, watching as she finally manages to tighten her skates, her fingers working the laces with determination. She looks up at me, a triumphant grin on her face, and I lean down to press a quick kiss to her lips.

"Ready?" I ask, offering her my hand.

She takes it, her grip firm but hesitant, and we step onto the ice together. At first, Clara wobbles, her legs unsteady as she tries to find her balance, and I tighten my hold on her, guiding her along the edge of the rink.

"Okay," she mutters, her brow furrowing in concentration. "This is harder than it looks." She stumbles on the ice and reaches out her free hand to grab onto the side wall, a quick flash of panic on her face. "How are people just...doing this?"

I laugh, steadying her as she stumbles again. "It's all about finding your center of gravity. Keep your knees slightly bent, and don't lean too far forward."

"Yeah, easy for you to say," she grumbles, but there's a smile tugging at her lips. She wobbles again, and I catch her before she can fall, pulling her against my chest.

Clara looks up at me, her face inches from mine, and there's that spark again—the one that's been igniting between us since the moment we met. It's impossible to ignore, and I wonder, for the first time in a long time, how I'm going to survive without this.

"You've got this," I whisper, and she nods, her determination kicking in. We start to move slowly, gliding across the ice in a rhythm that feels natural, like we've done this in tandem a hundred times before. Clara's laughter fills the air, bright and unrestrained, and I join in, the sound wrapping around us like a warm blanket.

We spend a few hours at the rink, skating until our legs ache and our faces are numb from the cold. But it doesn't matter, because every second with Clara feels like a gift I didn't know I needed, or that even existed. And when we finally collapse onto the bench, breathless and laughing, I realize there's no turning back from this. Because I'm starting to fall.

"I think I'm getting the hang of this," Clara says,

grinning as she unlaces her skates. "I might be a natural."

"You're a lot of things," I tease, nudging her shoulder, and she rolls her eyes, but there's a blush creeping up her cheeks that she can't hide.

We grab hot chocolates from a nearby stand and sit by the plaza's fireplace, watching as the sun starts to dip behind the mountains, casting everything in a warm, pink light. It's perfect—too perfect—and I can feel the ache in my chest growing, knowing this won't last.

Clara leans her head on my shoulder, and I wrap an arm around her, pulling her close. "I never thought I'd be doing this," she says, her voice soft. "This was so unexpected and so far from what I planned."

I nod, staring out at the mountains, my thumb rubbing lazy circles on her covered shoulder. "Yeah."

We sit there, wrapped up in each other and the dwindling daylight, and I want to tell her everything. I want to tell her that I've never felt this way, that she's changed something in me that I didn't even know was broken. But the words stick in my throat, too big and too messy to say out loud.

So instead, I kiss the top of her head, letting the moment speak for itself, and for now, it's enough.

17

CLARA

THE VILLA FEELS DIFFERENT TODAY, like it's holding its breath. There's a stillness in the air, a heaviness that settles in my chest every time I catch Tom's gaze. We've been dancing around this inevitable goodbye for days, pretending it's not right around the corner, but now it's here, staring us in the face. Tomorrow, he'll be gone before the sun is up, and I'll be left with nothing but memories of these strange, wonderful twelve days.

I try to push the thought away as I step out of the shower, the steam clinging to the bathroom mirror, blurring my reflection. I wrap myself in a towel and pause, staring at the foggy glass. My heart feels like it's caught between two worlds—one where I'm with

Tom, and another where he's just another chapter in my story, one that ends tomorrow morning.

I pull on a sweater and some leggings, trying to ignore the sinking feeling in my gut. When I walk into the living room, Tom is already there, sprawled out on the couch with his laptop open, probably checking emails or catching up on work. He looks up when he sees me, his eyes lighting up with that soft smile that's become so familiar.

"Hey," he says, closing his laptop and pushing it slightly off his lap. "I was thinking we could go into town. There's this little bakery I read about that's supposed to have the best croissants."

I smile, even though it feels bittersweet. Tom has been packing every last minute with something special, unforgettable, as if we can fit a lifetime into a few short days. And part of me wants to keep doing that, to keep pretending like this doesn't have an expiration date mere hours away.

"Or," I say, lifting one shoulder casually, like I wasn't up half the night going on about this in my head, "we can stay in and...just be us."

Tom raises an eyebrow, his smile widening as he sets his laptop on the coffee table. There's a flicker of surprise in his eyes, but it's quickly replaced by something warmer, something softer. "Just us," he repeats, like he's testing the idea on his tongue. He leans back against the couch, watching me closely, and I can see the wheels turning in his head, the way he's weighing this unexpected shift in our plans.

"Yeah," I say, trying to keep my voice steady, even though my heart is thumping wildly in my chest. "I don't want to go anywhere. Not today. I just want… this. Us. Here."

It's the truth I've been dancing around since I woke up this morning, since I rolled over and found him there beside me, his hair tousled and his breathing even, and it hit me all over again that he's leaving. I'm leaving, too. There's no use pretending that another coffee shop or a stroll through town is going to make this any easier. I don't want to waste the last hours we have left pretending like we're just passing the time.

Tom sits up, his expression softening as he reaches out and tugs me down onto the couch beside him. His fingers brush against mine, tentative but reassuring, like he's saying he gets it without needing to say anything at all. "Okay," he says, his voice low and warm. "Just us."

There's something about Tom that feels so easy, so natural, and I don't know how to reconcile that with the fact that this is ending.

"I got you something," Tom says, grabbing a gift box from the side table. It's wrapped in Valentine's Day paper, different heart-shaped drawings covering the red background and glitter adorning some of them. It's obnoxious and unnecessary, and I feel like I'm about to cry. I look up at him and he's staring at me, his eyes searching my face for my reaction. "It's nothing, just—"

"Thank you," I whisper, trying to contain my tears. I slowly unwrap the box and open it carefully, unpacking whatever is inside with the utmost care, as if moving in slow motion would delay the inevitable. "You didn't have to."

He clears his throat and gives me a small smile. "It's nothing," he says casually, almost uncomfortably.

I gasp when I see he bought the mug I had eyed at the small market days ago, that day we ran into each other and he was on that call with his daughter. "Oh my god," I say, and I'm rendered speechless. The simple act of him buying me something feels strangely intimate, like he's trying to leave a piece of himself with me. "I went back to look for it the next day and they had sold it."

Tom chuckles, tucking a strand of hair behind my ear, sending shivers down my spine. "I knew you liked it, so I called the store and he found one hidden some-where. I hope—"

"I—I don't know what to say," I stutter. I look up and see the sincerity in his eyes, the way he's looking at me as if I'm his entire world. "Thank you," I manage, my voice shaking.

Tom gently places the mug on the side table and

cups my face in his warm hands. His thumbs brush lightly against my cheekbones, and I lean into the touch, closing my eyes as memories of our time together flood my mind.

He leans in, his lips brushing against mine tentatively, as if asking for permission. I close my eyes, savoring the feel of him, committing every sensation, every detail to memory. The way his stubble feels against my skin, the scent of his cologne, the way his hands cup my face as if I'm the most precious item he owns.

The fire is still crackling in the hearth, casting a soft glow over the room, and Tom pulls me closer to him, holding me like he's also trying to memorize the feel of me.

"I don't want this to end," he whispers against my hair, his voice cracking, and it's the first time I've heard him sound unsure, vulnerable.

I pull back just enough to look at him, my hands cupping his face. "I know."

We move together, finding our way to the bedroom, and it's slow, almost reverent, like we're both trying to make every second count. Tom's hands are gentle as they slide under my sweater, his touch sending shivers down my spine, and I lose myself in him, in the feel of his skin against mine, in the way he kisses me like he's never going to get another chance.

We undress each other in a slow, deliberate dance,

shedding layers until there's nothing left between us but skin and heat and the undeniable pull that's been there since the start. Tom guides me onto his lap, his hands steadying me.

"I want to see you," he says, and I sink onto him, the feeling of him filling me up so completely that I forget how to breathe.

He moves beneath me, his hands gripping my hips, and it's not just about the physical—it's about everything we've been trying not to say, everything we've been trying to avoid. It's raw and unfiltered, the kind of intimacy that leaves you exposed, and I cling to him, my fingers digging into his shoulders as we lose ourselves in each other.

"Clara," he groans, his voice rough, and I kiss him, swallowing the sound because I don't want him to finish that thought, whatever it is. I don't want to hear the goodbye that's hanging on his lips.

We stay like that for what feels like hours, tangled up in each other, and when it's over, we collapse onto the bed, our bodies spent and my heart too full. I rest my head on his chest, listening to the steady beat of his heart, and I try to ignore the tears prickling at the corners of my eyes.

"What happens now?" I whisper, my voice barely audible, and Tom's arms tighten around me, his chin resting on the top of my head.

"We figure it out, if you want to," he says, and I can

hear the determination in his voice, even though neither of us has any idea what that means. "We keep in touch, we...try."

I nod, but it feels like a promise I'm not sure we can keep. Still, I want to believe him. I want to believe that maybe this doesn't have to be the end.

18

TOM

THE ROOM IS STILL CLOAKED in darkness when I wake, the faintest hint of dawn barely starting to edge its way through the curtains. I lie there for a moment, my arm draped over Clara, her body warm and soft against mine, and I let myself just feel it—this stolen moment, this fragile, fleeting thing we've built together. Her breath is even, her face relaxed in sleep, and I can't help but stare, committing every detail to memory.

I know I need to get up. My flight is in a few hours, and I still need to pack the last of my things, but I can't bring myself to move. I've been dreading this morning since the second we agreed to stay in yesterday, since the first kiss we shared. There's a tightness in my chest, a heaviness that makes it hard to breathe, and all I want to do is pull her closer and pretend that we have more time.

But we don't.

Slowly, I slip my arm out from under her, careful not to wake her as I sit up, swinging my legs over the side of the bed. Clara shifts in her sleep, her hand reaching for me unconsciously, and it almost undoes me. I sit there, watching her for a moment, and I can feel the pull to lie back down, to forget about flights and obligations and everything waiting for me on the other side of this morning. But that's not real. What's real is the job I have to figure out, the daughter I miss more than anything, and the mess of my life that I need to sort out before I can even think about trying for something—-anything—more.

I get up, moving as quietly as I can, grabbing my clothes from the floor and pulling them on. My suitcase is by the door, half-open, and I start shoving the last of my things inside, the sound of the zipper too loud in the silence of the room. I glance over at Clara, half expecting her to stir, to wake up and catch me in the act of leaving, but she doesn't. She just sleeps, her face turned towards the window, and I feel a pang of guilt so sharp it almost knocks the breath out of me.

I don't want to leave her like this. Not without saying something, not without one last kiss, one last promise. But if I wake her up, I know I won't be able to walk away, and I have to. I have to figure out my life before I can even think about asking her to be a part of it.

I sit on the edge of the bed and reach my hand out to her hair, tucking a piece neatly behind her ear. She stirs and whatever I just did comes undone immediately as she turns to face me.

"Tom," she mumbles and reaches out her hand towards mine. I thread my fingers through hers and squeeze, one, two, three times.

"Sweetheart." I move closer to her face, my words low and calm. "I have to leave," I whisper, and the last syllable catches in my throat. She hums and nestles into the covers, as if she's in a drowsy state of mind, not quite here with me but instead somewhere else. "I'm going to miss you."

I take one last look at her, memorizing the way the morning light touches her hair, the way her fingers curl into the sheets, and then I turn and walk out, each step feeling like it's taking me further away from something I didn't know I needed until now.

"Me, too," I hear from the bed as I'm reaching the door, and then she stirs again, switching sides and falling back into a deep sleep.

The villa is quiet, almost eerily so, and my footsteps echo as I make my way to the front door. I hesitate, my hand to the knob, and for a second, I consider turning back, crawling back into bed and letting the rest of the world wait. But that's not an option. Not when there's so much I need to sort out, so many pieces of my life that need fixing.

I step outside of the lobby, the cold air hitting me like a slap in the face, and I stand there for a moment, the weight of everything pressing down on my shoulders. The sun is just starting to rise, casting the first pale rays of light over the mountains, and it's beautiful in a way that feels almost cruel. I shove one of my hands in my pocket, my breath fogging in front of me, and start walking toward the shuttle that's waiting to take me to the airport.

Each step feels heavier than the last, and I can't stop the flood of thoughts rushing through my mind—Ellie's face when I tell her about the trip, the way she'll ask a million questions about what I did, down to the minute, about the snow, about everything. She should have been here with me, and the guilt of that sits heavy in my chest. I haven't been the dad I want to be, and if there's one thing I know, it's that I need to figure out how to be better, for her.

The shuttle driver is waiting by the door, a cheerful older man who greets me with a smile. "Heading back home?" he asks, and I nod, my voice caught in my throat. Home. It doesn't even feel like a place anymore, just a series of airports and hotel rooms, the endless rotation of work and travel and never settling anywhere.

"Yeah," I manage, climbing into the shuttle and

sinking onto the seat. I glance back at the hotel, my heart twisting when I see the soft glow of lights through the windows. It's like I can still see Clara there, wrapped up in the blankets, and it takes everything in me not to tell the driver to wait, to give me just five more minutes.

The shuttle pulls away, and the building fades from view, and I'm left with nothing but the memory of her smile and the ghost of her touch. I lean my head back against the seat, closing my eyes as the scenery blurs past, and I try to focus on what comes next—my job, Ellie, the life I need to put back together.

The flight is a blur, the hours slipping by in a haze of sleeplessness and second-guessing. I watch the clouds outside the window, the world passing by beneath me, and all I can think about is the way Clara felt in my arms, the way she looked at me like I was something worth holding on to. I want to believe that we can figure this out, that maybe this isn't the end, but the reality is that there's a whole world between us, and I don't know how to bridge that gap.

I start typing a message, something simple, something that doesn't make me sound like a complete mess.

> Hey, I'm sorry I left without saying goodbye. I just

I stop, staring at the words, and then delete them. It's not enough. It doesn't say what I really want to say, what I'm not ready to admit. Because it seems fast, doesn't it? Only ten days to fall in love with someone? I close the app, shoving my phone back into the seat pocket, and lean my head back, closing my eyes.

19

CLARA

THE FLIGHT back home feels surreal. Not in the way that travel can sometimes feel like a blur, but in the way that nothing feels right. Like I'm living someone else's life, one that no longer fits.

"Girl," Sofía whispers in my ear. She's crouched down in the aisle with her apron still on, the lights just barely out after the dinner service on this interminable redeye back to Buenos Aires. "What the hell happened to you? You look like shit."

I met her during my first year as a flight attendant, having crossed paths with her during training, and later we had a few flights together very early on in our career. We became fast friends, bonding over funny passenger stories and failed relationship woes.

"Nothing," I say, tucking the airplane-issued blanket tight around my shoulders. It's freezing in the plane, always is, and somehow, I misplaced my hot water bottle at the hotel in Canada. Seems like a stupid metaphor for my life, if you ask me. "I'm cold."

"*Aha, okay,*" she says, rolling her eyes so far back into her head that I'm afraid she's going to faint. "*Ni vos te lo crees.* What happened?"

"I'll tell you when we're home," I whisper now, trying to keep my mind off of Tom for the time being. It was a very dramatic day—from the moment he stepped away, the only thing on my mind was him. "When's your next flight?"

"Not for five days," she says. "Do you want to come over for dinner tomorrow? I should be rested after a nap."

"Okay," I say, with no intention of following through, but knowing quite well that she will barge into my parents' house if I don't text her back.

When I finally arrive home after what felt like the longest flight, I drop my suitcase in the entryway and glance around the house. It's big but cozy, and usually makes me feel safe, but this morning it feels empty. With a sigh, I kick off my shoes, make myself a cup of coffee, and settle on the couch, clutching the mug Tom bought me from that little market like my life depends on it. I rub my thumb over its ceramic handle, and suddenly, memories flood back—the warmth of his hand, his laugh echoing across the room, the way he looked at me like I was all he wanted in the world.

For a moment, I consider calling him, just to hear his voice, to bridge the distance between us. But what would I say? I miss you? I think I might have fallen in love with you over these past few days? I'm not ready to admit that out loud yet—not to him, and maybe not even to myself.

For the rest of the day, I replay every stolen glance, every laugh, and every quiet moment, and it drives me insane. He's like a shadow, following me around as I try to get back to my routine, reminding me of what I let slip away. And, if I'm being honest, what I wasn't brave enough to fight for.

Instead, I call Sofía. If anyone can talk some sense into me, it's her.

"Hey," she answers, her voice a little groggy with sleep. It's early evening now, but you can't tell, the last of the long summer days still clinging. "Are you here?"

"No, just wanted to check if you were up."

"I'm up," she replies immediately. "Come over. The house's a mess and I haven't unpacked, but I have drinks, and we can order food, or go to the little restaurant you like around the corner."

An hour later, I'm sitting across from Sofía in her living room, a glass of white wine in hand and a look of concern mixed with excitement on her face. "What the fuck happened in Canada?" she asks, lifting her knees to her chest and wrapping one arm around them. The other remains in the air, the glass of wine sloshing around with her enthusiasm.

I laugh, but it's forced. "I met someone."

"Yeah, no shit." She laughs.

"Actually, more than met—let's just say it's…complicated."

Sofía raises an eyebrow. "Go on."

"His name is Tom, and he's…" I take a deep breath. "Everything I didn't expect to find on this trip. We're so different, but somehow, it worked? But he's got a whole life somewhere else, a daughter, and I have mine here. How could we possibly make this work?"

Sofía takes a sip of her wine, nodding thoughtfully. Her dark blonde hair moves with her and she narrows her green eyes at me. "So, you're telling me you're just going to give up because it's complicated?"

"The whole thing with Santiag—"

"No. I'm sorry, but no." She drops her legs to the floor and sets her wine on the coffee table in front of her. For a brief second, I think she's going to stand up and start pacing the length of the room, but instead, she turns to face me. "Fuck Santiago, and I mean it with all the love in the world. He was great, but he was an asshole and he didn't handle things correctly. And listen, he was right about following his gut, so maybe you need to follow yours a little, too."

I sigh, tracing the rim of my glass. "It's not that

simple," I retort. "He has a family to think about, a business... Like, I can't ask him to uproot everything to move here to just be with me. That's silly."

"You're assuming he'd have to," Sofía says, shrugging. "Have you considered that he might be feeling the exact same way as you? Look, Clara, I know you like stability and routine, especially after the few years you've had, but maybe it's time to shake things up a bit. Take a risk. What's the worst that could happen?"

I stare at her, the idea of it settling uncomfortably in my mind. Maybe she's right. Maybe it's worth the risk. But that doesn't change the fact that there are things here I need to do before I can think about building something new with Tom.

"Let me see him," she says as she extends her hand my way.

"No," I say firmly, but smile in her direction. "You're going to stalk him and then you're going to start liking his old photos like a weirdo, and I don't want to be associated with your lunatic behavior."

Sofía cackles but sits next to me on the couch as I navigate to the app where I have his profile already pulled up. It's mostly pictures of him when he was still paying polo, a few brand deals, and a very old picture of his small family from years ago when he was still married and Ellie was still a baby.

"Girl," Sofía says with a gasp and settles deeper into the couch. "What the fuck."

"I know," I say with a groan.

"No, but seriously," she adds as she scrolls through the thousands of pictures on his feed.

"*Ya se, Sofi,*" I repeat.

"*Boluda,* what are you waiting for? Just call him."

"Yeah? And then what? I have nothing to say to him."

"Bullshit. Stop sabotaging yourself."

Sofía's words echo in my mind long after I leave her place and head back home. The house is dark and quiet as I enter, and I slip off my shoes, head to the kitchen and pour myself a glass of water, staring blankly out the window at the empty street. The truth is, I've spent so much of my life staying in one place, building routines, keeping everything neat and tidy. But it's always felt incomplete, especially in the past few years. Now, for the first time, I have a reason to want more. I just don't know if I'm ready to dive into the unknown.

I check my phone, half hoping there's a message from Tom, something simple and unassuming like *I miss you.* But the screen is empty, and a hollow ache settles in my chest. Maybe he's already decided it was just a vacation fling, a holiday romance that shouldn't carry any more weight than that. After all, he has his own life on the other end of the world.

Sofía's voice nags at me as I stand barefoot in the middle of my parents' kitchen, the dim light of the fridge casting an eerie glow on an already cold space. *Stop sabotaging yourself.*

She said it so confidently, like it is the most obvious thing in the world. But Sofía doesn't really know what it feels like to be, finally, so tethered to the life I've built over the past three years, with my dutifully constructed walls that guard me oh, so well. And what, does she intend for me to blow past them just because it felt good to be with this man for a few days?

I scroll back to Tom's profile, staring at a photo of him standing in front of a horse, hearts in his eyes for that magnificent beast. My heart aches, a pang so deep it takes my breath away. His face is familiar now in a way that feels dangerous, like I've memorized it without even trying. I can hear his laughter in my head, feel the way his hands always found their way to mine, even when we weren't saying anything.

The sound of my phone buzzing on the countertop startles me, and I grab it instinctively, my heart racing. But it's not him, obviously. It's Sofía, sending me a series of texts that make me groan.

SOFÍA

Did you message him yet?

Because if not, I will.

I mean it. Stop being a chicken shit.

I type out a quick reply.

ME

Leave me alone.

Her response is almost immediate.

SOFÍA

Never. Now call him, or I swear I'll do it myself. And you know I will because I'm a special kind of crazy.

20

TOM

RETURNING to New York feels like stepping back into a life that doesn't feel like mine. Even with my daughter here, it feels stifling. Clara's presence still lingers in every corner, a constant reminder of the warmth and laughter I left behind.

I go through the motions on autopilot, picking Ellie up from school or her mother's house on alternating weeks, heading to the office and planning out travel for the rest of the year. Until one day, three weeks into this sham I'm trying to call a life, everything snaps.

Robert drones on about expansion opportunities and a sponsorship deal that's been in the works for months. I nod along, but my mind is elsewhere. Clara's face flashes through my thoughts as I sit in meetings, as I scroll through endless emails, as I shuffle papers that mean nothing to me.

"You've been quiet," my business partner says one gray afternoon, snapping me out of my haze. The street down below looks dreary: people moving fast, clutching their coats and heading inside away from the cold. They all look miserable. "This is a big deal. We need your input."

I glance at the presentation on the screen. So much corporate jargon that I want to puke. When did this become my life? None of this matters.

"Robert," I say, standing abruptly. "I need to step out for a minute."

Robert blinks at me, confused. "We're in the middle of—"

"I'll be right back," I mutter, already walking out the door. My hands are shaking as I shove them into my pockets, pacing the hallway outside the conference room. The three people inside are looking at me like I'm a lunatic. And I partially feel that way.

This isn't my life anymore. I thought it was, for years. I thought the traveling and being with the horses—in whatever capacity—it all mattered. But now, this feels like a cage, and the worst part is that I built it myself.

The thought burns through me as I stand there, my breathing shallow and my hands trembling in my pockets. For weeks, I've been pretending I can just fall back into this life, as if Clara didn't change everything. Like she didn't open my eyes to how much more I could have, if I was brave enough to take it.

I stride back into the room and grab my laptop. Robert looks up, startled and very confused. "What are you doing?" he asks, halfway to standing, almost like he's about to stop me.

"I'm done," I say, my voice calm but resolute.

"Done with what?" he recoils, crossing his arms in a defensive way.

"With this. The business, the meetings, the traveling. All of it." I shove my laptop into my backpack, ignoring his sputtering. "I'm out, man. You can buy me out or I'll sell my share to someone else. There have to be interested buyers. I'm not doing this anymore."

"You can't just walk away," he snaps, his voice rising. "We've built this together."

"I know," I say, finally meeting his gaze. "And I'm beyond grateful for what we've accomplished, but this doesn't fit me anymore. I need something different."

My heart pounds as I step into the elevator, adrenaline like I haven't felt in a long time coursing through me. For the first time since *her*, I feel alive.

By the end of the day, I've signed an offer on a small plot of land in Southampton, tucked between a golf club and a winery, with a little house and stables that have seen better days and are just enough to start boarding horses. It's nothing like the sprawling polo fields I once called home, but it feels right. Like the kind of place where I can start over.

And that night, almost as if fate has intervened, a notification pops up.

SOFÍA

Hey. You don't know me. I'm one of Clara's friends. She's miserable and she's too afraid to tell you. So I'm helping her a little.

I stare at the message, my heart lurching.

ME

How bad is it?

SOFÍA

Bad enough I'm DMing you.

Her words hit me like a punch to the gut. Here I am, spinning my wheels, too scared to reach out and she's feeling the same way.

I close the app and stare at the ceiling, my thoughts racing. I've spent weeks trying to convince myself that it was just a fling, that we were just two people in the right place at the wrong time. And that she couldn't possibly be feeling the same things I was feeling for her, because it's more than that. More than a vacation flight or a misbooking gone wrong.

I grab my phone again and open a new conversation. My fingers hover over the keyboard, the words forming and reforming in my mind. I hit send before I can overthink it, my heart pounding in my chest.

21

CLARA

"Welcome aboard," I say, probably for the one hundredth time so far today. The hum of the plane's engines is a familiar comfort as I stand near the entrance, greeting passengers as they trickle on board. The routine is second nature by now—smiles, nods, assisting with bags too heavy to lift, answering questions about seat assignments and arrival times. I've done this a thousand times before, but today, there's a strange restlessness simmering under my skin, a weight I can't shake.

I steal a glance at my watch. The flight's delayed by nearly an hour, and the passengers are getting antsy, shifting in their seats and tapping their phones, sending off last-minute texts before we close the door.

It's the usual chaos, but it feels heavier today, and I know exactly why it is.

"Did you see the weather reports?" María Marta, one of my crewmates, asks as she leans against the bulkhead. She's in her fifties, with a soft demeanor and kind eyes, the kind of woman who always knows when to pass along a word of comfort. She's been doing this job long enough to have seen it all, but she still approaches every flight with the same quiet enthusiasm. "Apparently, there's a storm coming in later tonight. We're lucky we're not going west."

"Yeah, I saw," I reply, forcing a smile. "I guess that's why everyone's in such a rush."

María Marta nods, giving me a knowing look. "*¿Estás bien?* You've been a little quiet today."

I shrug, offering her a half-hearted smile. "Just tired, I guess. You know how the New York flights exhaust me."

It's not a lie, not really. I am tired—tired of the endless flights, of pretending I'm fine, of replaying those twelve perfect days in my mind like a movie I can't turn off. Every night since Tom left me sleeping in that bed weeks ago, I've gone back to that villa in my dreams, felt his arms around me, his breath on my neck, and every morning I wake up to the empty space beside me, the lingering scent of him on the sweatshirt I kept already fading.

"Alright, crew," the gate agent's voice crackles over

the radio, interrupting my thoughts. "We've got one more passenger running down the jet bridge. Just scanned in, so hold the door for a minute."

I nod, even though she can't see me, and I glance over at María Marta. "One last passenger," I say, trying to sound upbeat. "Always one."

María Marta laughs softly, shaking her head. "Always."

The moment stretches as we wait, and I find myself lost in the familiar dance of anticipation—waiting for the last passenger, waiting for the next city, the next flight, the next moment that might bring something new. I fiddle with my uniform, adjusting my name tag, and let out a breath, reminding myself to stay focused.

"Here they come," the gate agent's voice echoes again, and I look up, expecting to see another frazzled business traveler or a tired parent dragging their kids along. But what I see instead hits me like a bag of bricks.

Tom.

He's running down the jet bridge, his bag slung over his shoulder, his hair a disheveled mess from the wind. He's out of breath, his eyes scanning the plane as he reaches the door, and when he sees me, his expression shifts—relief, hope, something so raw and real that it knocks the air out of my lungs.

"Tom?" I breathe, my voice barely a whisper, and

he looks at me like he's been searching for something and has finally found it.

"Clara," he pants, his chest rising and falling as he catches his breath. "I—"

"Sir, you need to take your seat," María Marta cuts in, her voice gentle but firm as she gestures toward the cabin. "We're about to push back."

Tom holds up a hand, not taking his eyes off me. "Just a second, please."

The cabin is buzzing with impatience, passengers craning their necks to see what's holding up the departure, but all I can see is him—standing there, in front of me, like he's just walked out of my dreams and back into my life. I want to ask him why he's here, how he found me, what he's doing on my plane, but the words stick to my throat, tangled up with everything I've been too afraid to admit.

"I'm sorry," Tom says, his voice low and urgent. "I know this is crazy, but I had to see you. I couldn't just—"

"Sir, please," María Marta urges again, but I hold up a hand, silencing her. I need to hear him out. I need to know why he's here, why he's risking this.

Tom takes a step closer, his eyes locking onto mine. "I've been a mess since I left. I thought I could just go back, figure things out on my own, but every minute without you felt wrong. I kept thinking about everything we said, everything we didn't say, and I realized I don't want to figure it out without you."

My heart is pounding so hard in my chest, I can barely hear him over the rush of blood in my ears. I want to reach out, to touch him, to pull him close and never let go, but we're on a plane, at my place of employment, surrounded by passengers and crew, and I don't know how to make sense of any of this.

"You didn't have to come all the way here," I manage, my voice cracking. "You didn't have to do this."

Tom shakes his head, a determined glint in his eyes. "Yes, I did. I didn't want to leave things the way they were. I don't care about the distance, about the complications, about any of it. I lo—"

"Sir, please take your seat," María Marta interrupts, her patience wearing thin. "We really need to close the door."

Tears well up in my eyes, and I blink them back, overwhelmed by the intensity of the moment.

"I'm going, I'm going," Tom says, holding up his hands in surrender. He looks at me one last time, his expression a mix of hope and fear. "Please, sweetheart."

He turns, heading down the aisle to find his seat, and I'm left standing there, my heart in my throat, my mind racing. I feel María Marta's hand on my shoulder, a reassuring squeeze, and she gives me a knowing smile. "You okay?"

I nod, but I don't know if I'm okay or if I'm about to break apart. "Yeah," I say, my voice unsteady. "I think so."

"That's one love declaration if I've seen one," she says, fanning her face. Her eyes are shining with what I assume are happy tears, and I laugh, a wet sob coming out of my throat in surprise and... I don't know what.

The door finally closes, the plane lurches forward, and I watch as Tom settles into his seat, his eyes still searching for mine. The flight attendants go through the safety demo, and I try to focus, but all I can think about is him—right there, just a few rows away, and the way he looked at me like I was the only thing that mattered.

When we're in the air, cruising at ten thousand meters, I make my way down the aisle, my heart thundering in my chest. Tom looks up as I approach, his expression softening when he sees me. I kneel beside his seat, ignoring the curious stares of the passengers around us, and for a moment, we just look at each other, both of us caught in this impossible, beautiful bubble.

"I love you," I whisper, and Tom smiles, his hand reaching out to take mine. "I don't know how it happened or when, but..."

"I love you, sweetheart," he whispers back, leaning

towards me and tucking a strand of hair behind my ear like he's done many times before. It's wildly unprofessional, but I don't care. "I don't think I can live without you."

"You really came all this way?" I whisper back, straightening my back so that at least this appears less of an intimate conversation and just business as usual.

"I told you," he says, his voice thick with emotion. "I'm not done with you yet."

I laugh, a choked disbelieving sound, and squeeze his hand.

"We'll figure it out," he says. "One day at a time."

He leans forward and places his forehead on mine. "Never been so glad to be misbooked in my life."

EPILOGUE

A YEAR OR SO LATER...

CLARA

THE PLANE TOUCHES DOWN SMOOTHLY, its wheels humming against the tarmac, and I feel the familiar jolt of excitement I get every time I land in New York. The city's energy seems to seep through the walls of the airport, to the passengers moving hastily through the aisle, gathering their belongings and leaving in a rush to explore this wonderful city.

I pull my carry-on from the overhead compartment, smiling politely at the cleaning crew ready to turn over this plane. My muscles ache from the overnight flight, and my eyes are gritty from lack of sleep, but none of it matters. Not the long hours in the air, not the endless customs lines, not even the good-natured ribbing from my coworkers about my secret life in New York. Because at the end of every flight, there's Tom.

It's been over a year. A year and a half of weekly flights between Buenos Aires and New York, a year of stolen days and quiet moments that feel like they belong in another world, far removed from the routine of my everyday life. A year of learning to love him— not just in the big, obvious ways, but in the small ones, too.

The way he leaves the porch lights on for me, even though I always get there in the morning when it's already light out. The way he makes me coffee just the way I like it, even though he's turned into more of a tea guy in the past few months. The way he listens when I ramble about passenger stories or Sofía's latest relationship drama, his steady, calm presence grounding me.

I shuffle off the plane, my uniform wrinkled everywhere. The airport is bustling, the kind of organized chaos I've learned to navigate with ease. But today feels different. There's a fluttering in my chest, a sense of anticipation I can't explain.

When I clear customs and step into the arrivals area, I spot him instantly. Tom stands tall in his tan coat, his brown hair catching the soft autumn light filtering through the terminal windows. But it's not just him—it's Ellie, too, her auburn curls pulled back in a ponytail, bouncing as she waves at me excitedly.

For a second, I'm frozen in place. They've never met me here before—Tom usually waits for me at the house, especially on weeks when he has his daughter with him. My hand tightens on the handle of my suitcase as I move towards them, my heart swelling at the sight of both of them standing there together with their matching smiles.

"Clara!" Ellie shouts, breaking into a run in my direction. Her voice echoes in the terminal, and people turn to look, but I don't care. I stopped caring exactly a year ago when I thought I had missed the biggest thing to ever happen to me. I drop my bag just in time to catch her as she barrels into me, her arms wrapping tightly around my waist. She smells faintly of shampoo and hay, and I laugh, my exhaustion melting away.

"Hey, honey," I say, squeezing her tightly. "What are you doing here? Shouldn't you be in school?"

"It's teacher development day," she explains matter-of-factly, pulling back to look at me with her big, curious eyes. "Dad said we had to come because it's a special day."

"A special day?" I glance up at Tom and scrunch my nose. He's walking towards us, his hands shoved into his coat pockets, a sheepish grin tugging at his lips.

"Hi, sweetheart," he says, his voice warm and the corners of his eyes crinkling in that way that still makes my stomach flip. "She insisted, and I wasn't about to argue."

Ellie grabs my hand and pulls me towards him. "You're staying the whole weekend, right? Dad said maybe you can help me with Jupiter. He keeps trying to eat my hair."

I laugh, casting a questioning look at Tom. "Is that what you named the new horse? I thought you were going to name him Polo."

Ellie rolls her eyes and looks at her dad, shaking her head with a smile on her face. "No, ew," she says. "How predictable is that?"

Tom's grin widens and he reaches out, brushing his hand lightly against mine, his touch sending a familiar warmth through me. "You up for a day at the stables?" he asks softly, his gaze searching mine. "Ellie's got it all planned out."

"I can't think of anything better," I say, and I mean it.

The drive out of the city is filled with chatter—mostly Ellie's as she fills me in on everything I've missed since my last visit two weeks ago. Her voice is animated as she recounts Jupiter's latest antics, the progress she's made in her polo lessons, and the Halloween decorations she's been begging Tom to put up. I steal glances at Tom in the driver's seat, one of his hands steady on the wheel and the other one draped casually over my knee, his expression soft as he listens to his daughter. This is the life he's built, the one he's let me step into piece by piece, and I feel a swell of gratitude that I get to be part of it.

By the time we pull up to the stables, the autumn colors are on full display. The trees surrounding the property are all a picture of oranges, yellows and reds, their leaves carpeting the ground and making it look golden in the early morning light. The air is crisp, carrying the faint scent of hay and manure, and the familiar sight of the barn and paddocks fills me with a sense of peace I didn't know I needed.

After a short nap, I make my way down to the kitchen, where Ellie and Tom are eating. After lunch, the day passes in a blur of easy moments—helping Ellie with Jupiter's routine, wandering the paddocks with Tom, catching up on the little things that make up our separate lives. It's simple and quiet, the kind of day that feels like it belongs to us alone.

Later, as the sun begins to dip below the horizon and Ellie heads to her mom's house for dinner, Tom takes my hand and leads me to the edge of the property. There's a large oak tree there, its branches stretching wide against the sky, and a blanket spread out beneath it.

"What's this?" I ask, my heart picking up pace as he guides me to sit beside him.

"We're going on an adventure." He shrugs, his lips

curing into a small smile. "Just wanted to spend some time with you."

I laugh, leaning against him and sighing, because that's all we do when I visit. Almost like he puts his life partially on hold just to savor the precious hours we have together.

We sit there for a while, the silence between us comfortable, the colors of the early sunset painting the landscape in soft, warm hues. Tom's hand finds mine, this thumb brushing over my knuckles, and I lean closer to him, closing my eyes and letting the moment settle around us.

"I've been thinking," he says after a long pause, his voice low and steady.

"*Ay, no,*" I tease, glancing up at him. "That sounds serious."

He chuckles, but there's a nervous edge to it that makes me sit up straighter. He shifts, reaching into his jacket pocket and pulling out a small box. My breath catches, and my heart leaps into my throat.

"Clara, sweetheart," he begins, his eyes meeting mine, earnest and full of emotion. "This past year...it hasn't been easy. The flights, the distance, the juggling of schedules—it's been exhausting. But it's also been the best year of my life, because it's been with you."

Tears prick at the corners of my eyes as he continues, his voice growing steadier with each word.

"I've watched you fit into my life with Ellie, with

the horses, with everything I thought would scare someone off. But you didn't run. You stayed. And I can't imagine doing any of this without you."

He opens the box, revealing a simple, elegant ring that catches the fading light. "Will you marry me?"

For a moment, all I can do is stare at him, my chest so full it feels like it might burst. Then, without hesitation, I throw my arms around him, laughing through my tears.

"Yes," I whisper against his ear. "A million times, yes."

Tom pulls back just enough to look at me, his grin wide and boyish as he slides the ring onto my finger. "Good," he says, his voice thick with emotion and his eyes shiny with unshed tears. "Because I wasn't going to take no for an answer."

We stay there under the tree, the world around us fading away, and finally it feels like the last piece of the puzzle missing in my life clicks into place.

FIN

ACKNOWLEDGMENTS

This whole story was born because the main character, Clara, shares a name with my IRL sister. Clara (my sister) was slightly offended with the story arc I gave Clara (the character) in *After the Fire*, so I wrote it better. I really hope you like it and that I've redeemed myself...

Menace Chat and Sprint Baddies: I will keep thanking you until my fingers are raw because I wouldn't have written as much if it weren't for your encouragement. Thank you, Menaci, for supplying answers to millions of questions and for always indulging me.

Hailey: you took me under your wing almost two years ago and never let me go. Thank you for everything you're doing for my career, and for being the greatest friend one can have.

Lau y Kari: thank you for being my long-distance champions, always there to support me in any way I need. Siempre.

Presidential Es: Las mejores, obvio! Your friendship

means the world to me. I'm so glad we found each other in 2024.

Ellie and Keri: Thirty seven thousand words are not enough to express my gratitude for you. This story looks wildly different than what you originally read because your comments made it much, much better.

Bekah, Kait, and Lucile: Thank you for beta reading, for reacting and responding and egging me on. Your comments made me laugh and cry and helped me believe in this story.

Katie and Bobbi: My wizard editors that turned an okay draft into something magical. Thank you, always.

To my family, especially my husband, for giving me the gift of time to sit down with my characters so I could help them get their well-deserved Happily Ever After.

To my daughters: I hope that, eventually, my writing encourages you to pursue what you are passionate about, even if it doesn't work out at first and you have to keep on trying.

And last but not least, to my readers and my author friends: *Misbooked for Love* was a very hard book to write for many different reasons. 2024 was a tough year for me as an author but you were always there, engaging with me and encouraging me to keep going, even when it took longer than expected. Thank you. I hope you love these characters as much as I loved writing them.

ALSO BY MARIA RIGOU

Tres Fuegos Series

After the Fire: An Enemies to Lovers Small Town Romance

Before the Storm: A Second Chance Small Town Romance

ABOUT THE AUTHOR

Maria Rigou US-based author hailing from Argentina. She infuses her stories with the vibrant spirit of her heritage while exploring the complexities of love and relationships.

She lives in South Florida with her husband and two daughters and loves to read.

Misbooked for Love is her third book.

————

CONNECT ONLINE
www.mariarigou.com
@mariarigouauthor